the Wedding Planner's Secret

Wedding Bliss, Book 1

USA TODAY BESTSELLING AUTHOR

MELISSA McCLONE

The Wedding Planner's Secret
Wedding Bliss (Book 1)

Second Edition

Original version published as *His Band of Gold.*

Cover by Alt 19 Creative

Cardinal Press, LLC
October 2023

PROLOGUE

"You know what this means, don't you?" The beaming princess bride, Her Serene Highness Christina Armstrong de Thierry of San Montico, didn't give Kelsey time to answer. "You'll be the next one to get married."

"No." Kelsey Armstrong Waters stared at the breathtaking all-white royal bridal bouquet in her hands. The sweet scent of the roses tickled her nostrils as if the flowers got the joke. The last thing she'd intended to do was catch this stupid bouquet, but before she knew what was happening, she had. Her first thought had been to let the flowers fall to the ground, but as maid of honor—not to mention a wedding consultant herself—she couldn't allow that to happen. Nor would she allow herself to believe the silly myth. Not even for her favorite cousin. "I won't be getting married."

"You say that now." Christina gazed longingly at her handsome husband, Prince Richard de Thierry, and her smile widened. "Just wait until you meet Mr. Right. Trust me, you'll change your mind. Fast."

Kelsey didn't want to spoil her cousin's perfect wedding day, so she held her tongue. The institution of marriage might be perfect for Christina and many others, but it would never be for Kelsey. "Why don't you toss the bouquet again so someone else can catch it and not ruin any…traditions?"

"You won't be able to stop this tradition from coming true." Christina floated with joy in the crowded ballroom. Given her fairy-tale romance and royal wedding, no one could blame her, Kelsey included. Even the most cynical would have had a hard time not getting caught up in the magical atmosphere. No doubt this couple *would* live happily ever after. Christina sighed. "There's something about the magical power of love."

Magic was one thing, but love?

Forget it.

Kelsey knew firsthand that most marriages were doomed for failure—her parents and many of her clients were a part of the statistic. Marriage was as easy as saying "I do," but divorce was even easier. All that took was an "I don't" and a signature on the dissolution-of-marriage paperwork. A sad but true fact of life. And one she never wanted to be a part of. Ever. "I only caught the bouquet. I didn't get a royal engagement ring stuck on my finger like you did."

"Doesn't matter."

As Christina gave a royal wave with her left hand, the enchanted ring that had brought her and her prince together acted as a prism, sending a colorful spectrum of light flashing through the room. The sparkles landed ethereally on wedding guests as if the ring were spreading its magic on all it touched. Kelsey took a step back to avoid being hit, but the light still managed to glint on the bouquet in her hands. Better the flowers than her.

"You won't have any choice," Christina continued. "One day, your own Prince Charming will enter your life, and the next thing you know, you'll be married."

That only happened in fairy tales. And for Christina. Kelsey couldn't help but smile at her cousin's good fortune. But *she* was another story.

Kelsey was open to casual dating, but marriage?

No, thank you.

Too much hassle.

Too much trouble.

Too much heartache.

She tightened her grip on the bouquet. "Don't forget, I'm never getting married."

"Never say never." Christina grinned. "Trust me on this one, okay?"

Chapter One

January 31

A perfect match.

At her office, Kelsey Armstrong Waters stared at her reflection in the three-panel mirror and grinned. The vintage lace veil her friend Serena James, wedding dress designer extraordinaire, had found in London looked as if it had been woven specifically for the pearl, diamond, and porcelain flower wreath Kelsey found in Paris. That was why Serena was in such high demand these days—she knew what worked together.

A satisfied feeling settled in the center of Kelsey's chest. She adjusted the veil slightly to ensure it fell exactly as it should on whichever of her brides would wear the exquisite pieces.

Oh, my. Kelsey blinked. Once. Twice.

The unbelievable happened.

She looked like a radiant bride and felt like one, too. She could almost imagine herself getting ready on her wedding day even though she never planned on getting married. Still… Love, happily-ever-after, and even magic seemed to fill the room.

An unexpected rush of emotion overtook her. Kelsey sighed.

Serena had mentioned this happening when clients found their wedding dresses. Other dress designers and boutique owners had said something similar. But Kelsey thought it was hyperbole or an inside secret for those involved with the gown side of weddings. Now…

Was this how all those brides felt when they found "the" gown to wear? Was this the tingling inside that caused emotion to swell, tears to dot their lashes, and their smiles to widen? Was this it?

She took a deep breath and smelled the sweet scent of roses, but that wasn't possible. The only roses in her office were the dried blossoms from the royal wedding bouquet she'd caught last year and then had preserved to display for her clients to see. If anyone asked her, the one perk for catching the flowers was the pop culture value of having a piece of history from the royal wedding.

Thinking about the bouquet brought her cousin to mind. No doubt Christina would laugh if she saw Kelsey right now. On second thought, Christina would probably be thrilled and tell Kelsey what a lovely bride she'd be when she finally walked down the aisle herself.

But that wasn't about to happen. Not even

catching the wedding bouquet or wearing the breathtaking headpiece would change what she already knew in her heart to be true.

Marriage wasn't for her. Not now, not ever.

Frowning, she stared at her reflection once again. Trying on the headpiece had been a stupid idea. Her friends would be laughing so hard if they saw her, which was why she would not be taking a selfie to send to Serena, Jane, and Elle on their group chat. They'd never let Kelsey live this down.

She blew out a breath. "Why didn't I just eat a two-pound bag of peanut M&M's instead?"

"I prefer the original myself." The one hundred percent male voice sent a shiver down her spine.

Having a suite of offices in one of the most exclusive buildings in Beverly Hills afforded her some security, so she was surprised but not frightened by the voice.

Kelsey turned.

Standing in the doorway of the reception area was a man dressed in a pair of khakis, a white oxford shirt, and a brown leather jacket. Casual yet classic. A man's man kind of outfit. And that hair…

His deep brown—almost black—hair fell just above his jacket collar and was brushed back off his forehead as if it were a careless afterthought.

He was, in a word, spectacular. Considering her aptly earned title, "Wedding Consultant to the Stars," that said something. He could have been a model except for the slightly crooked nose, which gave his face personality. Lots of personality.

Kelsey smiled. His chiseled cheekbones could have only been sculpted by a great artist. His full lips hinted at hot, slow kisses, and his eyes made her feel as if she were the most important woman in the world.

This is the man I'm going to marry.

The thought came from out of nowhere, striking her like a bolt of lightning. She tried to understand the motivating factor behind it. Tried and failed. She'd been surrounded by gorgeous men most of her life and knew better than to be taken in by a pretty face. Still, his relaxed stance and easy smile appealed to her on a gut level.

He'd hardly said five words, but his charm filled the expanse of her office. Too bad she hadn't heard bells when she first saw him; then she'd know…

Know what?

That she was acting like a teenager with her first crush?

"May I help you?"

"I'm looking for Kelsey Waters." His captivating smile showed off straight white teeth, and her legs turned to linguini. Okay, she was a sucker for a great smile.

"I—I…" Hoping to quell the butterflies churning up her stomach, she breathed deeply and exhaled. Slowly. She couldn't remember the last time a man—any man—left her so tongue-tied, and she didn't like it.

She was twenty-six years old, not thirteen. Time to get control. "I'm Kelsey Armstrong Waters."

"So, you're the one I've been looking for."

Her breath caught in her throat. *Breathe*, she ordered herself. *Just breathe.*

"How can I help you?"

"I need help planning a wedding."

Reality hit Kelsey, low and hard. The handsome stranger was a potential client—someone else's groom.

Disappointment shot through her. Not that she personally wanted a groom. Though maybe she could borrow him for a date or two.

What was she thinking?

Oh, boy, she needed a vacation more than she realized. Time away from nervous brides and jittery grooms and six-figure weddings. Only a few more hours until her flight.

She forced a smile. "And you are…?"

"Will." As he walked toward her, he grinned. The smile crinkled the corners of his green eyes and made him even more appealing. "Will Addison."

Addison. The name sounded familiar, but she hadn't met him before. She knew that for certain.

"Nice to meet you." She forced the words from her drier-than-dry mouth and extended her right arm. As his hand touched hers, electricity shot up her arm and straight down to the tips of her leather pumps.

Ignore the tingles. Concentrate on something else, anything else. Like his handshake. His handshake was solid, firm, as was the man in front of her. She was nearly five nine, but she felt almost petite standing in front of his six-foot-plus frame. Realizing she'd allowed the handshake to last longer than was appropriate, she pulled her hand away.

"Nice veil," Will said in that deep, warm voice of his. "You'll make a lovely bride."

A bride? Kelsey touched the top of her head. Great, she still had the headpiece on. She could only imagine how ridiculous she looked in the getup. He could have at least mentioned it when he walked in so she didn't look like such a fool. Kelsey removed the wreath and veil and set them on a nearby table. "I'm not getting married. Just trying them on. I like to keep certain one-of-a-kind items in stock for my clients."

"Whatever bride wears that veil will be one lucky lady."

The compliment warmed her cheeks. What was happening to her? She wasn't the blushing type.

"You said you need assistance planning a wedding. How can I help?" The words came out sounding husky, a way she hadn't meant them to sound.

"My sister's getting married and wants you to coordinate her wedding."

His sister. Kelsey's pulse picked up speed, racing faster than a car chase on the 101. The knowledge that Will Addison wasn't the groom-to-be filled her with a euphoric feeling, like she's just found out one of her weddings was going to be featured on *Weddings of a Lifetime.*

Stop. Now.

She was thinking nonsensically and needed to reel herself in. Marriage wasn't on her radar or bingo card. Her parents had soured her to marital bliss. Nothing would change that. If anything, the past few minutes reaffirmed how badly she needed a vacation.

Kelsey motioned him to the area where she consulted with clients. "Why don't you have a seat?"

"Thanks." Will sat in one of the overstuffed chintz-covered chairs. "Nice place."

"Thanks." He should have looked out of place among all the feminine décor and bridal accessories, but he didn't. And it annoyed Kelsey. This was her turf, her home-field advantage, so to speak. He could at least have the courtesy to seem uncomfortable among all the ruffles, ribbons, and frills. "So, when..."

As he picked up one of the bridal magazines from the table and set it back down, Kelsey caught a flash of gold. She glanced at his left hand. At the ring finger of his left hand. At the gold wedding band on his ring finger.

Married.

The man of her dreams was somebody else's husband.

Of course another woman had realized he was a keeper. Yet he had flirted.

Well, maybe not flirted, but he—

Stop it.

This wasn't like her. Not one bit. Will Addison

wasn't the man of her dreams. Such a man didn't exist. Kelsey, of all people, knew better than to engage in any sort of romantic fantasy. Not even for the briefest of moments. And definitely not with a married man. She straightened. "When is your sister's big day, Mr. Addison?"

"Friends call me Will."

"I'm sure they do." Business demeanor back in place, Kelsey pulled down the five-year calendar planner from a nearby shelf and flipped it open. "So, when does your sister want to get married?"

"February fourteenth."

"I'm already booked for next year."

"Not next year." As he leaned toward her, she caught a whiff of him. Soap and water and something woodsy. Whatever cologne he wore, he smelled good. Too good. Kelsey inched back in her chair until she could go no farther. She didn't need a PhD to know Will Addison was trouble. Big trouble. "This year."

"But today's the last day of January. That's only—"

"Two weeks away. It's short notice, but—"

"Sorry, not possible." With no regret, she closed the planner. It would be much better this way. Much better for her, that was.

"You have another wedding scheduled?"

Kelsey hesitated. This wasn't her problem, her fault. Yet the intense look on his face… "I did, but it was canceled after the bride met someone else."

The corners of his mouth turned up slightly. "You can coordinate my sister's wedding, then." He wasn't asking a question.

"I can't. Several clients offered to move their weddings up to Valentine's Day, but I decided to take advantage of the cancellation and give my staff a well-deserved vacation. Everyone's gone."

Hope brightened his eyes, making them sparkle like emeralds.

No, not jewels, Kelsey told herself, *but broccoli or AstroTurf or anything else green and unromantic. Remember, he's married. And even if he weren't…*

"You're here," he said.

"Not for long. I haven't had any time off in months. My flight leaves in three hours." Kelsey reached for a nearby pad of paper and a pen. "I can give you some names of other wedding planners, but at this late date—"

"You don't understand." He brushed his hand through his hair, giving it an even more careless look than before. "It has to be you."

"May I ask why?"

"Both my mother and my sister want it to be you." The desperation in Will's voice almost made her believe it was true. He was a good actor, really good.

"If it's so important to them, why didn't they come?"

His lips tightened, and he glanced at the pile of magazines. "It's…complicated."

It always was. "Mr. Addison, I'm about to leave the country for a much-needed vacation. I don't have time for complications."

He stared directly into her eyes, and Kelsey felt woozy. "My sister is Faith Starr."

Of all the nerve…

The thought of Kelsey's previous interactions—and futile wedding planning efforts—with the woman made her blood pressure soar off the charts. "Faith Starr?"

At least now Kelsey knew why Will Addison's name sounded familiar—he was a blood relative, a brother no less, of the world's worst client. It was all coming back to her, like acid reflux. Will was the oldest of the siblings who traveled the globe running the family chain of Starr Properties—resorts, hotels, and inns named for his mother—that catered to the rich, the famous, and the not-so-famous. Just as Starr Addison's husband, Bill, had used his wife's name for the family's real estate venture, Faith had taken her mother's name for her stage name to honor the woman who'd given birth to her.

Not that it made a difference to Kelsey after what she'd been through with the actor.

Nothing made a difference where Faith Starr was concerned.

Kelsey rose, barely able to contain the anger threatening to erupt more violently than Mount Vesuvius. She was an Armstrong and had been raised properly to follow etiquette and protocol, but one could only be polite for so long. "Get out of my office, Mr. Addison. Now."

He stood. "I understand why you're upset. Faith hasn't been the most reliable—"

"Your sister is nothing more than a spoiled starlet who strings along fiancés as if they were her personal puppets."

Faith Starr, actor extraordinaire and the world's most notorious runaway bride, had almost given Kelsey an ulcer—four times in the past three years. Faith was a perfectionist both in her craft and in planning her weddings. Never had Kelsey worked so hard with so little payoff in her life.

"I've planned four weddings for her. Count them: four." Kelsey raised four fingers. That was four too many. More business was one thing, but this? "I won't be involved in number five."

"Can't we talk about this? Work something—"

"Out. I have nothing more to say on this matter, so please leave."

"If you only understood the circumstances—"

"Look." Kelsey tried to keep her tone polite yet firm. "I appreciate that you came on behalf of your family. That's very…noble of you, considering my past with your sister. But nothing you say will change my mind."

His assessing gaze made her self-conscious. It was all she could do not to smooth her skirt and check to see if a piece of spinach was caught between her teeth.

His eyes twinkled, at odds with the tension. "Are you always so stubborn?"

"Out. Now." At least the band of gold wasn't the only negative thing about Will Addison. "Get out of my office before I call security and have you thrown out."

GROUP CHAT #1

Kelsey put away the veil and wreath, ignoring a sense of regret at having tried them on, which was ridiculous. It was a part of her job to try on items and make sure they went well together.

A glance at the time told her that she had a few minutes to finish up before she had to leave. Kelsey also wanted Will Addison to have had time to leave the building. She wanted to wrap up loose ends so she wouldn't have to work while on vacation. She was biding her time to make sure he would be well and truly gone, so she might as well let Serena know how perfect the veil was and update her friends. Though friends never felt like a true enough descriptor for what those three women meant to her. Kelsey was close with Christina, but they were family by blood. Serena James, Jane Dawson, and Elle Cavendish were family by choice.

Her sisters.

They'd met during recruitment their freshman year

of college as part of the same sorority pledge class and become sisters in every sense of the word. Even though Jane had to drop out of school and no one lived near each other, the four of them had stayed in touch over the years. That was the beauty of technology.

Kelsey typed a text.

Kelsey: *The vintage veil works perfectly with the wreath, Serena. Thanks.*

Elle: *Pic?*

Kelsey: *Not yet, but I'll take one when I get back from vacation.*

Elle: *I love the idea of vintage wedding apparel. Not that I'm ever getting married.*

Serena: *Give it time. Your heart needs more time to heal.*

Jane: *You deserve so much better than your ex.*

Kelsey: *He was the wrong guy, but nothing wrong with being single.*

Elle: *I like being single.*

Kelsey: *Same.*

Serena: *Don't you have a flight to catch, K?*

Kelsey: *Yes, but I was waylaid by a potential client. Told him no, and I'm getting ready to leave for the airport.*

Elle: *Safe travels. Hope you get to hang out with that Didier guy.*

Jane: *Take lots of pics in San Montico!*

Serena: *Have fun with your cousin.*

Kelsey: *Thanks. I'm hoping to digitally detox while I'm away, but I'll check in if I get the chance. If not, I'll be in touch when I get home.*

Chapter Two

Waiting for Kelsey to step out into the hallway was far from Will's idea of a good time, but he wasn't leaving until he had a chance to speak with her again.

The seconds turned into minutes, the minutes into an hour. How much longer before she left for the airport?

He stared at the door to Kelsey's office. No catchy name for her business, simply Kelsey Armstrong Waters, Wedding Consultant, in a script font. Too bad there was nothing simple about the woman herself.

He should have handled it better, but Kelsey had caught him off guard, and he wasn't a man used to being caught off guard. He didn't like the feeling one bit.

Really, Faith?

Will was going to kill her. He shouldn't have promised to oversee her wedding planning while she finished filming her latest movie. Faith had told him this would be easy. As easy as pushing an elephant into an elevator. And the wedding was the least of it.

Will was used to being around beautiful, wealthy, accomplished women and having them flirt, even pursue him. He tolerated such women; he was an expert at fending off their advances unless he wanted a little company. But it never went further than that. No one intrigued him enough to make him want more.

Until today.

Something had happened when he'd seen Kelsey's reflection in the mirror. He'd stood transfixed as if watching a piece of living art. Unguarded expressions had played on her face, and emotion clogged his throat. He'd felt as if he were trespassing, but he hadn't been able to stop staring at her. Tall and willowy, with long chestnut hair that shone and sparkled like each strand had been individually polished, she looked so young, so soft, so sweet. The wistful smile on her face had touched his heart, and he'd wanted to capture the moment. For the first time in a long while, he'd felt the racing of his pulse, the pounding of his heart. And he'd liked the way it felt. Liked it a lot.

When Kelsey had realized she wasn't alone, the glowing bride-to-be had metamorphosed into an icy, distant professional. No flirting, no fawning. She'd even called him Mr. Addison and kept it strictly business.

Yet when she'd realized he was Faith Starr's brother…

Talk about passion boiling under a cool façade.

Will couldn't believe the change in the woman. Flames had danced within the violet depths of her eyes, raising his temperature enough to melt the ice in his veins. She'd shown restraint, yet her anger had been clear. No amount of charm would ever change her mind. Forget the sweet talk, even his never-fail smile hadn't worked.

Will didn't get it. He always got what he wanted from women. Even with Sara.

Sara.

Will's gut tightened.

What was he doing? Being attracted to Kelsey was one thing—he hadn't spent the past eight years as a hermit—but he had no right to be intrigued by her. She wasn't simply another guest at one of his resorts; she was the woman he had to convince to plan his sister's wedding. His family, especially his mother, was counting on him to bring Kelsey to Lake Tahoe. He wouldn't let his mother down. He *couldn't* let her down.

The door to Kelsey's office finally opened. She stepped out, locked the door, and turned. The moment she saw him, her lips tightened. "What are you still doing here?"

Her above-the-knee gray tailored skirt and jacket hugged each curve. Will forced his gaze to focus away from her body and on her face. There was both a delicacy and a strength to her features. Her classic beauty would only improve over the years, and she didn't need all the makeup she wore. High cheekbones dusted with blush, full lips painted the color of a mouthwatering plum, and eyelids outlined with black liner. At least she hadn't tried to hide the small mole near the left side of her mouth. "You seemed upset. I wanted to apologize."

She stared down her perfectly shaped nose as if he were a mere peon. Fine by him. Will knew how to deal with women like that. He made a living catering to customers, to the whims of the wealthy guests staying at his family's resorts. He hadn't thought Kelsey fit that cold and shallow mold. She'd seemed more the warm and passionate type, but it would be easier this way. Much easier. "I also wanted to apologize for Faith. She's very sorry for what she put you through."

"Which time?"

"All four of them," he admitted.

Unblinking, Kelsey studied him. "You've made your apologies. Now leave."

"I don't blame you for being upset at Faith, but I wish you would hear me out. You didn't lose money on any of her weddings."

"No, your mother saw to that, but I lost something far more valuable—my time." Kelsey flipped her hair behind her shoulder.

Something in Will's chest twinged.

Ignore it; ignore her.

"And it hurt my reputation," she continued. "In an industry like mine, reputation is everything."

"Granted, but Faith has changed. She loves her new fiancé and is serious about getting married this time."

"Which of her latest co-stars is she engaged to?"

"He isn't an actor."

The news seemed to surprise Kelsey, but she continued to stare at the gilt-framed botanical print on the wall. "A director, then?"

"No. His name is Trent Jeffreys. He runs a nonprofit agency."

"A nonprofit?"

"Low-cost housing, affordable living alternatives. He's even got Faith volunteering on a few of his projects."

"So he's not in the business." From the prim tone of her voice, Kelsey still wasn't swayed. "I don't think having a two-week engagement shows any growth on Faith's part."

Will saw her point. "She's been engaged since Halloween."

"So why are you only coming to me now?"

Here was where it got tricky. Once Kelsey agreed to come with him, she'd learn the truth, but for now, that was family business and private. Will wished he could keep it that way, too. Thinking about what had happened to his mother was hard enough. He didn't want to talk about it. Might as well dangle the big carrot instead to see if Kelsey bit.

"As I said, it's the real deal this time. No more Hollywood extravaganzas like the weddings Faith asked you to plan for her. She and Trent want a small wedding with only close friends and family in attendance."

"Doesn't matter. At this late date, every place is booked for Valentine's Day."

"Not the Starr Lake Inn at Tahoe."

Kelsey's sharp gaze met his. "Weddings aren't allowed at Starr Properties."

"True. They are intrusive to our other guests, but rules are made to be broken. Especially for family." Will saw he'd piqued her interest. "Unfortunately, the plans for Faith's wedding have gotten—how should I put it?—a little out of hand. We aren't known for putting on weddings, and we need a professional like yourself to help us with the finishing touches and the final arrangements."

Kelsey said nothing. The seconds ticked by. Time to seal the deal. America knew how wealthy the Armstrong family was, so money wouldn't be a good motivator. But according to his mother, Kelsey's business meant the world to her. "If you agree to work on Faith's wedding, we'll allow you to use a Starr property for one future wedding. Any wedding."

Kelsey's eyes widened. Yes, her interest was genuinely piqued. Leave it to his mother.

"I'd want an exclusive contract to use any Starr property."

Will was used to negotiating with cutthroat realtors, city planners, you name it. Sharks, all of them. Kelsey was just as sharp and smart. And something told him he would enjoy the challenge. Will smiled. "Only one?"

"At least one at each of your properties."

Ouch. The shark bit off one of his limbs and spit it back at him. She reminded him of his mother, who was the reason the resorts were such a success. She had taught him everything she knew about business and negotiating. His mother had also taught him when to cut bait. "Fine. You may put on one wedding at each property, provided you work with my office and use our chefs and staff."

Kelsey got a faraway look in her eyes that softened the features on her face, reminding him of how she'd looked when he first stepped inside her office and saw her in the veil. "Let me get this straight. All I have to do to get this wonderful opportunity is cancel my vacation, go with you to Lake Tahoe for the next two weeks, and work on Faith's wedding at a resort?"

"Yes."

"I don't think so."

He did a double take. "What did you say?"

"I said no." She adjusted the leather bag on her shoulder. "Not even the exclusive use of Starr Properties could make me want to work with your sister again. You know that saying, fool me once, shame on you, fool me twice, shame on me. What does it say about me when I've allowed someone to fool me four times? There's no way I'll be fooled a fifth. Now, if you'll excuse me, I have a plane to catch."

Kelsey pushed past him.

Her strength of will impressed him. At least she had principles. But everyone had a price. He only had to find hers. "What would change your mind?"

She pursed her lips. "Do you have another sister who wants to get married?"

"Hope's already married."

"Sorry."

But he could tell she wasn't. He'd never expected her to turn down his offer. Now, he was in a real bind, which left him only one other option.

To tell her the truth.

"Wait."

She turned. "What is it now?"

"There's something I haven't told you about why we need you to plan Faith's wedding."

"That doesn't surprise me."

This was hard. Much harder than he thought it would be. Will tugged on his now-too-tight collar. "My mother was the one coordinating and making all the plans."

"Then you don't need me. Starr's amazing. She could plan any event with her eyes closed."

Kelsey was right on the mark about his mother. Starr Addison could do anything she put her mind to, except the one thing that had become her all-consuming goal: marrying off her youngest daughter.

"That was before," he forced the words out.

"Before what?"

"My mother had a stroke, and she…" Swallowing hard, he pulled himself together. "She said the only one she trusted to pull off the wedding she'd planned for Faith is you."

CHAPTER THREE

Starr? A stroke?

It wasn't possible. But the gravity in Will's gaze told Kelsey it was true. Tears stung her eyes, and she blinked them away. She might not be a fan of the daughter, but Starr was an amazing mother and person. The woman was thoughtful and generous, too. Kelsey had enjoyed working with her each time Faith planned a wedding.

"How is she doing?"

He shrugged, his features tight. "Things are progressing…slowly."

A stroke. Kelsey didn't know what to say. She remembered the helpless feeling that had engulfed her and her entire family when her grandmother Waters had suffered a stroke. The long days and endless nights until Grandmother had had another stroke and died. Kelsey fought the urge to offer comfort. He had a wife to do that.

"I'm so sorry. I truly am."

"Thanks." His voice was deeper than she'd heard before, and he glanced at the ceiling. "It's been a…difficult time for all of us. Faith wanted to postpone the wedding, but my mother insisted it go on as planned. Mom tried to continue doing all the work herself, but it was too much for her."

Too much for Starr Addison?

Kelsey tried to imagine Starr as anything other than her vibrant and energetic self, a woman who'd even tried snowboarding last year to see what it was like. A strong, confident woman who still had an Achilles' heel—her daughter Faith.

Each time Faith decided at the eleventh hour to cancel her wedding, Starr would break the news to Kelsey and hand her a generous check for the work she'd done as if money could wipe the slate clean. Starr apologized for the inconvenience, but not once had she apologized for her daughter's actions. Neither had Faith, for that matter. Kelsey chalked it up to family loyalty. Still, a simple "I'm sorry" would have made such a difference, but none had come.

She'd kept waiting and hoping. Of course, she'd only contributed to the situation by continuing to plan Faith's weddings, mostly because Kelsey enjoyed working with Starr, but she wasn't going to give in and do it again.

Kelsey really wanted—no, she *needed* to take a vacation. Just her reaction to Will suggested she needed to get away from her daily routine. Designing wedding after wedding without time for herself or a little male diversion had taken a toll. A couple of weeks on the island paradise of San Montico with her cousin Christina was exactly what Kelsey needed. A little rest and relaxation. She thought about what Jane had texted her about Prince Richard's royal advisor, Didier Alois. Maybe he'd forgiven her for turning down his marriage proposal, and they could spend some time together. If he hadn't, making up would be a nice challenge. She enjoyed his company, even if he'd gone a bit far by proposing after only knowing her for one week. A casual flirtation would be fun.

Yes, this vacation was what she needed, craved, deserved.

"I'm really sorry, Will, but I have a plane to catch."

"My mother's only wish is to see Faith married. It's more important to her than her own recovery." He gazed straight at Kelsey, making her feel as if she needed to take a step—make that ten steps—back. "And you're the one she wants to help her."

An invisible noose tightened around Kelsey's neck, but she needed to resist caving in. The last thing in the world she wanted to do was to plan a fifth wedding for Faith. Kelsey had promised herself not to allow Starr to sweet-talk her into doing another wedding for her daughter. Now, it wasn't only Starr asking, but Will, too.

"What do you say?" He shifted his weight from one foot to the other. "Will you help my mother make her dream come true?"

A grapefruit-size lump of guilt lodged in Kelsey's throat. Closing her eyes, she thought about her grandmother and how important dreams had been to her. Dreams she'd had for each of her grandchildren and shared with them before her stroke. But the stroke had taken away those dreams, taken away everything. There had been little time to do anything but say goodbye. Kelsey had wanted to do more, so much more. She'd missed that chance. Maybe helping Starr would ease some of Kelsey's regrets.

The ding of a bell announced the arrival of the elevator, and the doors opened.

"Your staff is on vacation, but I'll help you." Will smiled. "Tell me what you need done, and it'll be done. I don't know much about weddings, but I'm a fast learner."

Her eyes sprang open, and her heart leaped with pleasure at the thought of being near Will. The feeling was totally illogical, downright ridiculous. Forget about not wanting to work on Faith's wedding. The last thing in the world Kelsey wanted to do was to spend two weeks working with Will Addison. "Faith will want to work on her own wedding."

"She's on location and won't be flying in until the day before the wedding. She made me promise to oversee things until she arrived."

This didn't sound like the Faith that Kelsey knew. The starlet wanted to be involved. She'd overseen everything down to the flower arrangements for the last wedding. Starr was always a big help, but even she demurred to her daughter's wishes. "Faith trusts you to oversee her wedding preparations?"

"Yes." A wry grin graced his lips. "Do you have a problem with this?"

Kelsey's stomach twisted and turned and tumbled. She should have eaten more than a croissant for breakfast. "Of course not. I've worked with grooms—men—before."

"Does this mean you'll do it?"

"I…" Glancing at the closing elevator doors ahead of her, she watched her vacation disappear. And with it, her stress level inched upward.

"You can't imagine what it will mean to my mother and my entire family."

Grrr. She didn't want to work on another wedding for Faith. Kelsey had promised herself she wouldn't, yet for her grandmother and Starr… "Okay."

"Okay, what?"

"I'll coordinate Faith's wedding." The gruffness of Kelsey's voice should have bothered her, but it didn't. She was doing this under duress. "I'm not saying it again."

"I'm not asking you to." Will grinned. He was practically dancing like a bride-to-be registering at Tiffany & Co.

At least one of them was getting some enjoyment out of this. It wasn't her. She wouldn't be happy until

February fifteenth—when Faith's wedding was over and done with, and Kelsey was back home. "I want an exclusive contract to plan weddings at Starr Properties. As many weddings as I want."

"Fine."

"And my normal fee went up." Money meant little to her, but she wanted to make them pay. This seemed as good a way as any. Unlocking the door to her office, Kelsey stepped inside. "Way up."

He followed her in. "Okay."

Nothing about this was okay. She was mentally prepared and physically packed for a beach vacation. Now, she would have to pivot completely to go from vacation mode to wedding planner mode. That gave her an idea.

"Hey, I just had a thought." She forced a smile. "I could plan the wedding remotely."

He shook his head. "My mother wants you there. Tonight. So if we could get going…"

Ugh. She blew out a breath.

"I need to pack a few things here. I'll also have to stop by my condo, repack my suitcase, and make a few phone calls." She paused, wondering if she could make him change his mind about taking her with him. Not the fairest way to play, but she was desperate.

"It'll take a little while. I understand if you don't want to wait."

"I'm happy to wait."

Ugh. He was just trying to make her happy. Kelsey

was tempted to ask him to jump just to see if he would. She set her bag on the reception desk instead. With no warning, Will touched her shoulder, sending shivery sensations shooting up and down the length of her arm. "You don't know how much this means to me."

"Let's get one thing clear." She moved away from him, from his much-too-pleasurable touch. She'd brushed off advances from a few of the most handsome actors and musicians in the business—some even grooms-to-be. That had been bad enough, but this was much worse. Will was married. M-a-r-r-i-e-d. "I'm not doing this for you. I'm doing it for your mother."

And my grandmother.

"I understand."

Kelsey shook her finger at him. "And I swear, if Faith doesn't get married this time…"

"I know my sister." He smiled. "She's getting married on February fourteenth."

Kelsey flashed him one of her give-me-a-break looks. "Care to make a wager on it?"

His eyes gleamed as if amused by the idea. "It's a sucker's bet."

"I happen to like suckers." She grinned. "Lime's my favorite."

"Cherry happens to be mine."

"So I'm tart, and you're sweet." She laughed. "This could make for an interesting wager."

He smiled. "Seriously, there's no need for us to bet.

Faith will go through with it this time. Trent's different from her other fiancés. What you see is what you get. No games, no ego trips. Faith has found the one."

"The one?" Kelsey tried not to sound too incredulous.

"Her soulmate, heart mate, love of a lifetime."

Surely, he couldn't be serious. Yet the wistful look in his eyes was hard to ignore. It must be the lighting, right? Men didn't get wistful about such things. Especially married men. Yet a part of her wondered if Will had married who he believed to be his "one" and how he treated her because he sounded completely in love with his wife.

Kelsey tucked a strand of hair behind her ear. "Don't tell me *you* believe in those things?"

"Of course, I do." His eyes narrowed. "Just because I'm a guy doesn't mean I'm not…"

"A romantic at heart?" she offered.

He nodded. "There's nothing wrong with being romantic. Women like that in a man."

Kelsey shrugged. "Some women might, others…"

"I feel sorry for those who don't."

Oh, boy. They came in all shapes and sizes, those romantic idealists who believed in love at first sight and happily ever after, but she'd never met one in a more perfect package than Will Addison. Too bad she didn't share any of his beliefs.

No, it wasn't too bad. After everything she'd been through growing up, Kelsey knew better. That reminder should kill whatever attraction she felt for

Mr. Romance.

She headed toward the storage room. "Would you give me a hand, please?"

Together, they carried the leather trunk she took with her to out-of-town weddings into the office. From Telluride to Turkey, the contents of that trunk had saved the day more than once.

Will tapped the top of the trunk. "What's this for?"

"Anything I might need to keep me from having to run around a town I'm not familiar with and waste time I don't have to spare. You'd be amazed at what can happen on the morning of a wedding."

She opened the trunk, rummaged through it, and made a mental list of what needed to be packed. "Does Faith have a wedding dress to wear?"

"Yes."

"That's right. I forgot," Kelsey said. "She's got four of them. Let's hope she hasn't had any alterations done yet in case she's a no-show again."

Will laughed. At least he had a sense of humor. Not that it mattered, she reminded herself.

"Does she have a headpiece and veil?"

The smile faded from his face. "My mother planned to make one herself, a la Martha Stewart. She got hooked on crafting last summer, but the stroke…"

"I've got plenty to choose from." Kelsey stared at her selection. "Do you know what style of gown Faith's chosen?"

"No," Will admitted. "That's been the most highly guarded secret, next to her engagement itself."

"Not a problem." Kelsey filled the trunk with a variety of headpieces—halos, silk flower wreaths, beaded tiaras, and veils of all different lengths. If worse came to worst, she'd call in a few favors owed to her. "We'll bring several with us."

"What about the one you were wearing?"

It would kill her to let Faith wear the vintage ensemble, but Kelsey had to admit it would look lovely with the movie star's long, wavy locks. "I'll pack it."

"Do you need anything else in here?"

She gathered up a couple of garters and guest books in case Starr hadn't gotten around to that, either. "Would you grab the lavender toolbox in the storage room?"

"A toolbox?"

"Tricks of the trade." And right now, she needed every trick she had up her sleeve to get through packing her gear with Will's help. If it felt strange here in her own office, she didn't want to think about what it would be like working with him in Lake Tahoe.

"What tricks would those be?"

"Sewing needles, thread, safety pins, first-aid kit, clear nail polish, hair spray, things like that."

"You're very prepared."

"I have to be. My clients expect nothing less. I do my best to make sure their wedding day is the happiest, most perfect day of their lives."

He stared at her with an odd look on his face. "A person's wedding day is only the first of many happy days."

Using all her willpower, she managed not to roll her eyes. "Wasn't your wedding day your happiest day ever?"

Her question seemed to catch him off guard, but only for a moment. The sweet smile on his face made Kelsey swallow hard and remind herself he was already taken.

"Yes, it was the best day of my life." The dreamy tone of his voice touched a place deep within her heart.

His wife was a lucky woman. Or would be, until the marriage unraveled and fell apart. They usually did. No doubt they hadn't been married long or faced many bumps in the matrimonial road. "Told you so. Every person deserves a perfect wedding day, even your sister."

Will stared at Kelsey. "You take what you do very seriously."

"If I didn't, I wouldn't be doing it."

"So you're a romantic at heart, too?"

"No, not at all." She smiled at the ridiculous notion. No one she knew would ever call her romantic. "I'm just good at my job thanks to being organized and disciplined. Having a fail-proof checklist and my toolbox hasn't hurt. But in all honesty, I've become one of the best in the industry without a romantic bone in my body. I'm more of a…realist."

A realist, she thought, who knew the truth—there was no such thing as "happily ever after."

GROUP CHAT #2

Kelsey hadn't planned on texting her friends while she was in San Montico with Christina, but she wanted to let them know her itinerary had changed in case something went wrong or there was an emergency.

Kelsey: *Hey, change of plans. I'm now taking a two-week detour before I head to San Montico.*

Serena: *What?*

Jane: *Where are you going?*

Elle: *Are you okay?*

Kelsey: *Remember that guy I mentioned? I changed my mind about doing his event. What's one more wedding before my vacation, but the event is hush-hush. When I can say more, I will.*

Serena: *I hope you're sure because you needed a break.*

Jane: *Please don't overdo it.*

Elle: *Maybe the four of us can do a girls' weekend this spring or summer. You're still going to need a vacation at some point.*

Kelsey: *Oh, let's plan on that. I would love for all of us to be together again.*

Chapter Four

Sitting in the living room of Kelsey's condo in Brentwood, Will tried to make sense of the woman who'd agreed to coordinate Faith's wedding. Kelsey hadn't said yes out of the goodness of her heart. She would be well paid and receive an exclusive contract to put on weddings at Starr Properties. But he'd seen her genuine concern over his mother's condition. The tears in Kelsey's eyes, the slight quiver of her lower lip, the crack of her voice.

From the doorway of what Will assumed was Kelsey's bedroom, she leaned out, a toiletry bag in one hand, a phone in the other. "I'll be a few more minutes. Would you like something to drink?"

"I'm fine, thanks."

Watching her pack a trunk of wedding paraphernalia in her office had been like watching a professional golfer win The Masters Tournament. Not one motion wasted, not one hit in a bunker. In her apartment, she was no different and made multitasking look as effortless as a stroll along the greens on a spring morning. "Do you need any help?"

"No, thanks."

This didn't surprise him. He'd never seen a more self-sufficient, organized woman before. No wonder his mother had been so adamant about his bringing her back with him. "Let me know if you do."

"Okay." With that, she was gone.

Strictly business. Minimal exchanges. Polite manners. That was how Kelsey had acted for the past hour. He should be pleased. Yet, Will couldn't forget the look of pure joy on her face when she'd tried on the veil or the flirtatious smile and the way she'd batted her eyelashes when she'd first seen him. She was a contradiction. That much he'd discovered in the short time they'd known each other.

Will settled back on the couch. Obviously, there was more to Kelsey than met the eye. She was professional and smooth on the outside. He could only wonder what went on inside.

He was very good at reading people. Over the years, he'd learned to anticipate the needs and wants of their guests by listening to them and piecing together things he heard, just as his mother had when she'd convinced his father to buy the Lake Inn so many years ago. That ability made Starr Properties successful. But Will had trouble figuring out Kelsey. Dressed in her designer clothes with perfectly applied makeup and the right amount of jewelry and accessories, she could be any one of his guests; she might have even been one at some point in time. But she was unlike any of them, and it bothered him that he noticed.

Regardless of his attraction to Kelsey, or whatever it was, Will had to concentrate on Faith's wedding. That was what really mattered, the only thing that mattered.

In two weeks, his sister would be married, his mother would be happy, and the intriguing wedding consultant would be out of his life. Two weeks. Only fourteen days. He would make it. He would get through this, as he always did.

Will stared at the pictures covering the walls and on the fireplace mantel. Most were photographs of the Armstrong family comprised of politicians, lawyers, doctors, and corporate elite. They were darlings of the paparazzi, and one of the closest families to royalty America had. The most recent photo—resembling a family reunion with numerous aunts, uncles, and cousins—had been taken in front of the San Montico royal palace.

Last summer's wedding had been the social event of the year and was broadcast live all over the globe. Mom had gushed over the fairy-tale romance and asked Will to wake up early to watch the wedding with her. He'd said no, much to her regret then, but he didn't want to see another couple find their happily ever after. Not when he'd lost his. Yet he'd punished Mom for the way he felt. That hadn't been right, and he should've known better.

Even after losing Sara and realizing how important family was, he'd taken his parents' and sisters' love for granted. At least he had until Mom's stroke. Now, he realized how fleeting time was. He was determined to show everyone he loved how much they meant to him, no matter the cost. That was why he was in Beverly Hills and why he wouldn't leave without Kelsey.

Kelsey reappeared in the doorway. "If you're bored, there are magazines in the ottoman. I'll be ready in a few minutes."

Before he could say anything, she disappeared again. Will opened the ottoman that doubled as a coffee table. Inside, he found stacks of magazines ranging from *Bride* to *Vanity Fair*, a few novels, and some photo albums.

Curious, Will removed one of the albums. Opening the cover, he saw it was more of a scrapbook than a photo album, containing everything from actual wedding pictures to newspaper and magazine clippings about various weddings. As Will flipped through the pages, he recognized the extent of her clientele. But something else happened, too.

An unexpected warmth filled him. Kelsey had surprised him yet again. She might not consider herself a romantic, but one thing was clear. Someone who put this much time and effort into preserving the memory of each wedding she coordinated had to be sentimental.

Each two-page spread contained photographs of

the bride and groom and the reception and keepsakes from the wedding, such as a ribbon or ceremony program. Everything was neatly matted on coordinating paper, and she'd written captions under each item.

He continued paging through the book. Each wedding was different. From movie stars to political figures, Kelsey had managed to pull off spectacular and unique weddings for each of them. Some were enormous affairs with a security detail and media coverage, but others appeared to be more intimate gatherings. That made him happy and relieved since that was what his family was hoping for.

After he reached the end and put the album back in the ottoman, a satisfied smile formed on his lips. Taking Kelsey home with him was the right move. Beneath the all-business exterior was something warm and fuzzy. That was what they needed—correction—what his mother needed. And Faith, too.

Opening the next scrapbook, he expected to see more wedding memorabilia. He didn't. Will gasped. He jerked his hand away but then forced himself to continue. He turned one page and another. This book didn't celebrate her clients' marriages; it marked their divorces.

Will frowned. He couldn't believe what he was reading. Page upon page of clippings. Ugly accusations, tearful confessions, angry photographs. Her clientele was the kind to get as much press coverage surrounding their divorces as with their weddings. In the upper corner of each page Kelsey had noted the years, sometimes only days, the marriage lasted. Will tried to reconcile the first book with the second. He couldn't.

The first book showed how much she loved her job, and the photographs and clippings reaffirmed her talent for designing weddings, but the second scrapbook was the exact opposite. He didn't get it. Something didn't add up. He placed the book back in the ottoman and closed the lid.

Kelsey entered the room with one suitcase in her hand, another rolling behind her, and a bag on her shoulder. "I'm ready."

Will hesitated. Should he mention the scrapbooks? She was supposed to come home with him, but was it in his family's best interest to put her in charge of Faith's wedding? He wondered, after what he'd just seen. The divorce album rubbed him the wrong way and made him wonder if Kelsey had a hidden agenda or something. He felt as if he'd opened the cupboard of a health fanatic only to find a stash of junk food.

"Is something wrong?" she asked.

A perfect segue, but something held him back. Was he reading too much into this? Maybe the divorce album was a joke. Maybe he was too embarrassed to admit he'd peeked at her scrapbooks. Maybe he was looking for any excuse not to take her home with him and spend the next two weeks by her side.

"No." His goal had been to get Kelsey to coordinate the wedding as his mother wanted. It was what Faith had asked him to do. No sense changing course now despite his own reservations.

Will rose from the couch. "Let's go. Our plane is waiting for us."

* * *

Talk about a bumpy flight. Another wave of turbulence shook the Learjet. Kelsey checked her seat belt for the millionth time. Habit. Turbulence, she could handle. But Will Addison?

No matter which way she turned, she could see him, smell him, sense him. Talk about feeling claustrophobic. If only she had a parachute…

Kelsey didn't understand what was going on. Okay, that wasn't the entire truth. But the truth bothered her, made her feel lower than low. Not even worthy of being at the bottom of the food chain. Will might be Faith's brother; he might even be married. But Kelsey was attracted to him, attracted to his looks, his smile, and his easygoing manner.

And she hated herself for the attraction she felt.

She sank into the luxurious leather seat and leaned her head back. Married was synonymous with leprosy because in her book, Will was untouchable, off-limits, whatever you wanted to call it. She wouldn't be a catalyst for the breakup of a marriage. Kelsey would sooner gouge out her eyes than get involved with a married man. Which meant she had to ignore her attraction to Will Addison, had to ignore he was even a man.

She'd witnessed what infidelity could do to a marriage, to a family, thanks to her own parents. Her father had been the first to stray, but her mother had followed in his footsteps until eventually their world fell apart. She remembered the accusations, the fighting, the tears. But amidst her parents constant fighting, it was she and her brother, Cade, who had be the ones to lose. Worse, they'd become pawns in a vicious winner-take-all custody battle.

Will shifted in his seat and stretched his long legs out in front of him. His calf brushed hers, and a burst of heat emanated from the point of contact.

Ignore it, she ordered herself. Something told her she would be having to ignore many things over the next two weeks.

"So how did you become a wedding consultant?" he asked.

Thank goodness. A safe topic. Business-related, even. Kelsey counted her lucky stars. "My parents divorced when I was nine. When it came time for them to marry others, they both asked for my brother's and my input. I think it was their way of trying to make things easier for us. My brother couldn't have cared less, but I got into it. Each time they remarried—"

"Each time?"

"My father's been married eight times, my mother six, and she's currently engaged to number seven." It wasn't a big secret to anyone who knew anything about the Armstrongs. Many followed the happenings of America's second most famous family. "Needless to say, I had lots of practice planning weddings."

"Why did you pick Beverly Hills to open your business?"

"When I was thirteen, my mother married a producer, who moved us from Chicago to Beverly Hills and introduced me to the entertainment industry. He's husband number three and five."

Will's eyes widened. "She married him twice?"

Kelsey nodded. "And divorced him twice, too."

Will frowned. "Your family sounds a lot different than mine."

"I know. Your parents have been together forever. Starr was very proud of that."

Will smiled. "Divorce isn't mentioned in our house. No Addison has ever been divorced."

"None of them?"

"No grandparents, aunts, uncles, cousins, or siblings."

"That's…unbelievable."

"But it's true." Pride rang out in his voice, and Kelsey felt a stab of envy. "We've all been fortunate to find the right person."

"Not Faith."

"She hasn't married yet."

"You don't have to remind me." Kelsey stared at him. "So, do all members of the Addison family stay in miserable marriages to avoid divorce?"

"We don't have miserable marriages."

And there was a pot of gold at the end of every rainbow. She nearly snorted. "Seems to me most marriages end up that way eventually unless you're very lucky."

He raised a brow. "This from a wedding consultant?"

She nodded. "That's why I take my job so seriously. Every bride deserves to feel like a princess and every groom, a prince. The least I can do is give the couple a day to remember, a day to hold close to their hearts after things sour."

"Is that why you keep a scrapbook of your clients' divorces? Not one showing the successful marriages filled with pictures of babies and children that come from the ones that work?"

A mixture of embarrassment and anger washed over her, yet she contained her temper. Like it or not, Will was a client. And as she'd learned from her parents, blowing up over something that couldn't be changed never solved anything. She shrugged, but the last thing she felt was indifference. No one had ever seen her scrapbooks. Until that moment, she'd forgotten she'd put them in the ottoman instead of their usual hiding place. "Not many of the marriages I coordinate last."

"No doubt because of your 'Wedding Consultant to the Stars' moniker." Sarcasm laced his voice. "You haven't seen what real marriages are about, how good, how strong they can be."

"Is that how you feel about your marriage?"

"Yes."

She'd seen too many failed marriages to believe the Addisons had the market cornered on happy ones. "You think you found your soulmate?"

"I have no doubt."

Kelsey heard the conviction in his voice. Such a romantic. She couldn't ignore her curiosity about his wife, the woman who'd captured Will Addison's heart. "How did you know she was the 'one'?"

He got a faraway look in his eyes. "It happened the day I met her."

Love at first sight? Talk about a fairy tale. This she had to hear. "How did you meet?"

Will glanced out the window at the red-streaked sky. The sun was setting slowly. "It was Sadie Hawkins day. I was in sixth grade. All the boys tied their names on their belt loops, and the girls chased us. If a girl managed to get your name, you were hers for the day."

Wow. He and his wife had been childhood sweethearts and were still together after all this time. Kelsey found that hard to believe. "Sounds…fun."

"For the girls ,maybe," he admitted with a soft smile. "Sara, my wife, was new to the school. I'd never really paid much attention to her before because she was so shy and quiet." His voice trailed off.

"Go on."

He hesitated. "Sometime during the chase, one of the girls pushed her. Sara fell. Her knee was bloody, and she was crying. I went over to help her up."

"Don't tell me she grabbed your name tag?"

He nodded.

"And that's how you knew?"

He moistened his lips. "Sara held on to my name, and she smiled, a wide grin with a mouthful of braces, and I knew."

"Knew what?"

"That one day I would marry her." He glanced away. "And I did. Two days after I graduated from college. That was ten years ago."

"You were young."

"I wish I'd married her sooner."

"That's sweet." Saccharine, even. How could he feel that way after ten years? Longer if one counted how long they'd been together. Maybe he'd gotten lucky, like his parents and grandparents.

His eyes glimmered. Tears?

Kelsey found that almost as hard to believe as being married forever. Maybe he wore contacts and had a piece of grit in one of his eyes. That would explain it.

"I'm looking forward to meeting her," Kelsey said to break the silence.

"You can't meet her." The green of Will's eyes darkened, and his lips tightened. "Sara…passed away. She was killed in a car crash eight years ago."

Chapter Five

The air whooshed from Kelsey's lungs. Oh, no. Was there a worse time to put her foot in her mouth?

She struggled for a breath and the right—appropriate—words to say. She could handle even the most awkward wedding situations, but this had left her speechless. Not wanting the uncomfortable silence to stretch any further, she settled for the most obvious yet overused sentiment. "I'm so sorry, Will."

"Thanks."

No pain in his voice, no anguish on his face, but that didn't make her feel any better. Okay, his wife had died eight years ago, not eight days, but Kelsey felt about a quarter of an inch tall. From everything he said about love and marriage his heart still belonged to one woman and one woman only. "I hope I didn't—"

"You didn't."

"I thought since you wore a wedding band…"

"It's okay, Kelsey. Really."

She nodded, trying to believe him and not wanting

to say another word. Her brother would have a good laugh right now. Cade always called her Ms. Manners and teased her that she should write an etiquette book when she grew tired of designing weddings. So much for handling any situation with aplomb and ease.

The muted whine of the plane's engine filled the cabin and kept the silence from becoming unbearable. Kelsey straightened in her seat and dug the toes of her black boots into the carpet. They must be getting closer to their destination. Yet each passing minute felt like an hour. She'd never heard Starr or Faith mention Will being a widower. They'd never even mentioned he'd been married. Questions about him filled Kelsey's mind. She wanted to know the answers, but she didn't dare ask.

Will appeared to be in his early thirties. If Sara was his soulmate and one true love, did that mean he planned to spend the rest of his days alone? Kelsey wasn't sure whether his answer would make him the world's biggest romantic or biggest fool. Surely, he must have loved Sara—*must still love her*—if her memory was enough for him. But Kelsey found it hard to believe anyone could love another person that much.

Will cleared his throat. "Once we arrive, we'll head to the Lake Inn. You'll have the use of one of our suites."

"Thank you." The edges of Kelsey's mouth turned up slightly. "You must have been confident I'd come if you saved me a room."

"Let's say I was hopeful. Tonight, you can unpack and get settled in. We'll have breakfast at my parents' house and start work tomorrow."

She hesitated. Her next statement required the right amount of tact.

"I appreciate your offer to help, but I'm sure the time it would take will be a huge inconvenience to both you and Starr Properties to spend the next two weeks working with me."

He chuckled. "I appreciate your concern, but Starr Properties has been doing quite well these past few months without me working eighty hours a week. My staff knows how to find me if they need anything. And you know Faith. She'd kill me if I didn't keep her informed about everything you were doing. Trust me, it will be easier if I'm completely involved."

Easier for whom?

Faith, sure.

But what about Kelsey? A free-fall descent onto a parking lot might be easier to survive than spending the next fourteen days with Will.

No, she was simply overreacting. He'd caught her off guard. That was all.

Working with Will Addison wouldn't be difficult. So what if he was interesting? Charming and handsome, too. But he was also a die-hard romantic. Kelsey wouldn't want to touch a man like that with a ten-foot, make that a twenty-foot pole. Not even a slight flirtation appealed to her. She settled back in her seat and tried to convince herself that these next two weeks would be a snap.

The drive from the airport to Lake Tahoe's North Shore passed without incident. Night had fallen by the time Will pulled his SUV into the parking lot of the Starr Lake Inn.

Kelsey climbed out. Falling snowflakes greeted her, clinging like confetti. Her breath hung in the chilly night air. She tugged the front of her jacket together to keep from getting too cold.

When she faced the hotel, the sight warmed her. She almost thought she was in the Swiss Alps instead of the Sierra Nevadas, except for the larger size of the inn. Despite its size, the hotel exuded charm with its horse-drawn sleigh waiting for passengers. Its gingerbread-trimmed balconies on each of the floors were movie-set perfect but better than any set designer could fabricate on a sound stage because this was real.

She walked next to Will. About twenty yards away from the lobby entrance, she noticed two men talking to a bellhop.

Kelsey froze. Every nerve ending went on alert. Garrett Malloy and Fred Silvers were reporters/photographers for *Weekly Secrets,* a cheesy tabloid that reported on celebrities with an almost stalker-obsessive slant. If the dynamic duo caught sight of Kelsey and put two and two together, all bets for an intimate, private wedding would be off. She tried to stay out of sight. "We have a problem."

"Only one?" Will asked.

"No, two." Kelsey motioned to the men standing outside the entrance to the inn. "Sleazy tabloid reporters," she whispered. "They would kill for a scoop about Faith's wedding."

Will frowned. "I haven't told anyone except my personal assistant. There's no way they could have found out."

The two men walked toward them. If they came much closer, they would see her. Kelsey couldn't take the chance. She glanced at Will. "Desperate times call for desperate measures."

Kelsey wrapped her arms around him and nuzzled her face against his neck. Warmth emanated from him. Even though he wore a jacket, she could feel how solid he was underneath. And boy, did he smell good. Even better up close than before. She took another sniff.

His sharp intake of air brought her back to reality. She shouldn't be enjoying this as much as she was. She shouldn't be enjoying this at all.

"What are you doing?" Tension filled his voice, made him stiffen.

"Hiding."

"You're only bringing attention to—"

"Just go with it," she whispered, "for Faith's sake."

Will blew out a puff of air. As the sound of footsteps crunching on the snow grew louder, he pulled Kelsey closer. And closer.

One of the reporters snickered.

This wasn't going to work. The reporters would recognize her. Put two and two together and…

Will cupped her face and then covered her mouth with his own.

Oh, my.

The feel of his lips moving against hers made her close her eyes and moan. This was better than a kiss in a dream. Way better. Hot. Knee-meltingly hot. Soft. Purest-cashmere soft. And delicious. Mouthwatering-souffle delicious. She wanted more, so much more. Kelsey leaned into him, taking what she wanted.

"Get a room," a man—one of the reporters?—said.

Will deepened the kiss. The taste of him, the feel of him, the scent—all of it was intoxicating. She could easily become addicted to this.

Will stepped back so quickly that she nearly fell forward. She struggled to regain her composure, to make her heartbeat stop racing, to calm her ragged breathing.

"They're gone." He whipped out his cell phone and punched in a number as if the kiss hadn't had any effect on him.

She might as well have just run a hundred-yard dash at the equator. Her blood boiled. Her pulse raced. Her heart pounded. Not even the cold night air managed to cool her down. Never had she been kissed so thoroughly. And never had she been so shaken.

Will closed his cell phone. "They haven't been the only reporters hanging around."

She struggled to forget about the kiss, forget about the ache building within her. "C-could your assistant—"

"No." His lips tightened. "Confidentiality is a priority at every Starr resort. Besides, most people, including the guests here, think we're throwing a thirty-fifth wedding anniversary party for my parents, not a wedding."

Kelsey did a double take. The kiss had muddied her mind, her senses. "An anniversary party?"

"My parents were married on Valentine's Day," Will explained. "My mother thought it would be romantic to have Faith marry on the same day as she and my father did."

The dash of romance was enough to clear Kelsey's head and force her to focus on the task at hand. Maybe sharing the same wedding date would be enough impetus for Faith to follow through this once. "At least it won't look odd for Faith to fly in for the anniversary party."

Will stared at Kelsey. "But it will look odd for you to be here."

Remember, the customer is always right.

At least until she could get them to change their minds. Kelsey took a deep breath and exhaled slowly. "How am I supposed to coordinate a wedding without being on-site?"

"You can be on-site, but you'll have to keep a low profile. At least until the day of the event."

That, she could handle. "A couple of weeks of

room service won't be bad. I can work early in the mornings or late at night when the guests are still in their rooms."

Will furrowed his brow. "What about meeting with vendors?"

"I'll manage," she said. "I've worked on top-secret weddings before."

"But the press could find out."

"I'll stay at another hotel." She was used to last-minute changes. "If anyone asks why I'm here, I can say I'm scouting wedding sites. I'll rent a car and—"

"No." Will stared at her, his eyes cloudy. "You can stay with me."

"With you?"

"A path connects my house to the inn. It's a nice walk, and you can enter and exit through the service entrance without being seen by our guests or the press. It's the only thing that makes sense."

Only if one is certifiable. "I don't want to impose."

"You won't. The press will get bored waiting for Faith to show up, and then you can move into the inn. It'll be a few days at the most."

A few days. That didn't sound so bad to Kelsey as long as there were no more kisses. And why in the world would they kiss again?

"I'm sure it'll work out fine."

Chapter Six

Fine. Kelsey's definition of the word and Will's had to be miles apart. The only way to make things work out fine was to get away from her—ASAP. Will concentrated on his driving.

"Would you mind if I turned on the radio?" she asked.

"Go ahead." His voice sounded cool, even to him. "I also have Spotify with some playlists."

"Thank you."

So polite. Just an act, Will was certain. If she were truly polite, she wouldn't have kissed him back the way she had. Yes, he'd been the one to kiss her, but she'd been so passionate and eager. That shouldn't have happened when the kiss had been nothing more than an act, and he wanted to pretend he hadn't felt anything. Pretend this kiss was like the others had been since Sara's passing, fleeting and unmemorable. But based on his very real reaction, he didn't know if he could pretend.

Will didn't like that, didn't like the way Kelsey had made him drop his guard, if only for a rare moment. There had been other women in his life since Sara's death, but no relationships he considered remotely serious. Nothing he couldn't forget or live without. Nothing he'd wanted to take to the next level.

But with Kelsey…

It had only been one kiss, but holding her with their lips pressed together had felt like coming home. Home to a place he'd forgotten existed after years of exile. He wanted to go back. Again and again.

And that made absolutely no sense.

Sara was the only one who had made him feel that way.

As Kelsey scrolled through his playlists, he caught another tantalizing whiff of her perfume. The scent reminded him of her kiss. Passionate, seductive, hot. The perfume tickled his nose the same way it had during the flight from LA.

Will tightened his grip on the steering wheel. He should have bought a Hummer instead. The front seats had to be farther apart than the ones in his SUV.

Who was he kidding? He could be sitting at the opposite end of a widebody aircraft, and he'd still be able to smell her.

Her perfume, he corrected himself.

Will searched the recesses of his memory. He glanced at his wedding band and struggled to remember the fragrance Sara had worn. Something light. Floral, perhaps? Sweet and gentle as the woman herself. But he couldn't remember the scent, the name…nothing.

What was happening to him?

He should remember it, all of it.

"This is one of my favorites." Kelsey pushed *Play*.

The sound of blues filled the confines of his car. It was one of Will's favorites, too, but right now, anything would be better than music that brought smoky and sultry and seductive images to mind.

He shifted in his seat. At least they didn't have far to drive.

Once again, he questioned what he was doing. Kiss or no kiss, taking her home with him was pure insanity. Eight bedrooms and six bathrooms aside wouldn't be enough space with her in the house. Unfortunately, he didn't have a choice. The words had flown out of his mouth before he could stop them. An instinctive reaction. A way of changing what couldn't be changed.

I'll rent a car.

Sara had said those same words to him over the telephone eight years ago. They'd had a long-distance marriage while she was in graduate school. She'd flown home and arrived on time, but his flight from a business trip had been delayed. Not meeting him at the airport had dampened her spirits, but only for a moment. She was too excited about being finished with finals and spending an entire week with him. She'd offered to rent the car and leave his at the airport so he could make it home to her that much sooner. But a patch of black ice had changed everything. Ice had sent her rental sliding into oncoming traffic. Ice had taken her young life and ruined his.

Feeling the familiar tightening of his heart, Will flicked on the turn signal to make a right and turned off the emotion welling within him. He pulled into the long driveway and parked in front of his house.

Only two weeks and Kelsey would be gone.

Facing her, he pasted on his my-home-is-your-home resort-owner smile. "This is my house."

She stared at the house. "It's lovely. I expected to see a smaller version of the Starr Lake Inn, not a Victorian."

Across the wide expanse of the front porch, the golden hue of interior lights shining through the pane-glass windows radiated warmth. "My grandparents originally owned the house, then gave it to my parents for a wedding present. My mom and dad turned it into a B and B. The humble beginnings of Starr Properties."

"You grew up in this house?"

"Yes. My parents had another house built a few years ago and, following tradition, passed this house down to the firstborn. Traditions are big in my family."

"I'm beginning to see that." She smiled. "With all this snow, it looks like a winter wonderland. Something from a Thomas Kinkade painting. You know, your house would be a charming site for a wedding."

"This one isn't part of our deal."

"I meant Faith's wedding. Imagine if the bride and groom left in a horse-drawn sleigh."

"And you say you're not a romantic."

"I design weddings. By definition, weddings should be romantic. That doesn't mean I have to be."

One tough cookie. Will felt sorry for Kelsey. She didn't know what she was missing.

He slid out of the SUV and removed her bag from the back. A breeze blew through the trees, sending more snow to the ground. Will walked next to Kelsey along the path.

"Be careful." Snow covering the walkway crunched beneath his feet. "You don't want to slip."

"I won't slip." Confidence laced each of her words. He wouldn't have expected any less from her. "I've spent lots of time in cold-weather country."

He shortened his stride to match hers. Just in case. "Do you ski?"

"Excuse me?"

"You said you've spent time in cold-weather country. That usually means you ski or snowshoe or ice fish. You don't look like an ice-fishing enthusiast or snowshoer."

She wrinkled her nose. "I'm not. I ski."

"Cross-country or downhill?"

"Downhill. My family, the Armstrong side, spends part of the holidays skiing in Colorado. Every other year, my brother and I join them."

"And the alternate years?"

She pursed her lips. "We spend it with my father's side of the family."

"Have you skied recently?"

"To be honest, it's been a while. Work keeps me busy. People get married all year round."

"Thanks again for giving up your vacation to help us out."

She looked up at the dark sky. A snowflake landed on the bow of her lip, and she licked it off. "It feels good to be out of LA."

He'd been in Los Angeles for less than a day, but he knew how she felt. "Fresh air is good for the soul."

"Anything has to be better than inhaling smog."

"Why do you stay?"

"It's home," she admitted. "You get used to the traffic, the air quality, and the people after a while."

He could never get used to those things. Not when places like this existed. "You seem pretty normal for a SoCal resident."

She laughed. "I'll take that as a compliment."

"It was meant as one." Will took her elbow and helped her up the stairs.

"Thanks." Kelsey grinned. "Do you open doors and pull out chairs, too?"

"Always." He smiled. "My parents raised me right."

He opened the front door.

She stepped inside and gasped. "Oh, Will. This is absolutely beautiful. I can picture it now. Faith could enter down the staircase for the wedding ceremony. We can drape the banister with a floral garland. Very old-fashioned. Victorian, to match the house."

Will stared at her, trying to figure her out. He couldn't. "How do you do it?"

"Do what?"

"Picture exactly how a wedding will look. How beautiful, romantic, whatever, when you believe it'll make no difference in the long run?"

"It's a gift." Kelsey shrugged off her coat, and Will hung it on a coat rack. "Who do we have here?" Before Will could answer, she bent over and held her hand in front of Midas's nose, who sniffed her fingers. "You sure are a sweet kitty, aren't you? What's your name, handsome?"

"Midas," Will answered, not believing what he was seeing.

Midas meowed. He lapped up the attention and rubbed against her hand.

Will's chest tightened. Most people kept their distance from Midas with only three legs and scars not even his long orange hair could disguise. Yet Kelsey picked Midas up and held him as if he were no different than any other cat. She hugged him close. Nuzzled him. And Midas ate it up. He loved to be cuddled more than anything.

"Listen to you purr," she crooned. "Any louder and you'd need a muffler."

Will laughed. "Why do you think we named him Midas?"

Kelsey grinned at the cat. "And to think I thought everything *you* touched turned to gold." She kissed Midas's forehead and then placed him on the hardwood floor. The orange fur ball rubbed against her calf and wouldn't leave her side.

Not that Will blamed him. There were much worse things in life than rubbing against those long legs.

Will raised his gaze to hers. She stared at him unwaveringly, as if she knew he was checking her out and was curious about his assessment. He had to admit she was physically attractive. Not that he was interested in her that way. If only the voice in his head would stop laughing, stop mocking him. "I'll show you to your room."

"Thanks."

He followed her up the stairs and tried to ignore the sway of her hips. Everything about her oozed sensuality. She seemed interested in him. It would be so easy to make the most of these next two weeks, nothing more than a vacation fling since she would be leaving. But…

He couldn't.

Not with Kelsey. She was dangerous. Only a few hours in her presence had made his numb heart feel prickly as if a million pins and needles were trying to bring something to life that had been dormant for much too long.

"Do you mind telling me what happened to Midas?" she asked.

"He was in a car accident. He survived. Sara… didn't."

"Oh, Will."

He stopped walking. Memories from back then always made it hard for him to do more than one thing at a time. "At first, I hated Midas for living. He was never my cat. Always Sara's. I kept thinking, why couldn't he have died instead?"

Kelsey touched Will's arm. He ignored how good the small gesture felt, ignored how much he wanted, needed, to be touched. He concentrated on his cat and continued down the hall.

"But watching him recover… It would have been easier on him if he hadn't survived." Will rubbed Midas. "He's on his sixth or seventh life by now."

Will opened the door to what used to be his sister Hope's room. Faith still considered her old room to be hers and would want to stay there when she arrived for the wedding. Hope, on the other hand, couldn't care less where she slept as long as her three children were within earshot. "Make yourself at home."

"Thanks." Kelsey placed her purse on the bed. "Like everything else in the house, it's perfect."

Her compliment brought a smile to his face. "I'll carry your suitcase up to your room after I fix dinner."

"I'm not hungry, so don't go to any trouble."

"I won't."

His gaze met hers. He wanted to leave, but something held him in place. It was almost as if a thin cord connected them when it was only empty space. Still, he hadn't felt this way since…

No, he'd had his chance at love.

He wouldn't get another one.

Living alone wasn't so bad. He had his family and Midas; he had his work. Children of his own would have been nice, but that hadn't been in the cards for him and Sara. Still, he had two nephews and a niece. And once Faith married, maybe she would add a few of her own. That was more than enough for him.

"I'll freshen up," Kelsey said, finally breaking the silence.

"I'll be downstairs when you're ready." He stopped at the doorway to call for Midas only to watch the cat follow Kelsey into the bathroom. "Turncoat," he mumbled, feeling both betrayed and envious at the same time.

CHAPTER SEVEN

February 1

Standing at the front door of Bill and Starr Addison's not-so-humble abode with Will at her side, Kelsey had one question running through her mind. How had she wound up here? The obvious answer was via Will's SUV and, to take it a step further, by his plane. But the obvious wasn't what she was looking for.

Something was happening to her internally, and she didn't like it. This morning she'd woken from the strangest yet most sublime dream she'd ever had. A dream of fairy-tale weddings, magical kisses, enchanted bridal bouquets, and a groom who bore a strong resemblance to Will Addison. No doubt wearing the veil yesterday had fueled her subconscious, and the kiss they'd shared had stoked the fire, but what she was imagining—feeling—still made zero sense.

She wasn't the type to put too much meaning in dreams, if she even remembered them in the morning, but this one, she couldn't get out of her mind. Especially the thought of a smiling Will, waiting for her at the altar. This was so odd. She never got carried away by this sort of stuff.

Okay, that wasn't completely true. Kelsey *had* gotten caught up in San Montico's legend of the ring when the royal engagement ring was stuck on her cousin Christina's finger. The legend claimed whoever wore the ring was the prince's one true love, and that was exactly how it turned out. Christina had fallen in love and married the prince.

But that was a one in a million occurrence. Modern-day fairy tales didn't happen.

A bell rang. It took a moment for Kelsey to shake off her daydream and realize the bells were real—the result of Will pressing his parents' doorbell, not a bit of magic left over from the enchanted engagement ring.

Talk about relief.

The door opened.

"It's so good to see you again, Kelsey." Bill Addison greeted her with a hug. He was a more mature version of his son, with salt and pepper hair. Same smile, same eyes, same charm. "We're so happy you could help us with Faith's wedding. Starr is excited to see you."

At least *someone* was happy this morning. Kelsey forced a smile. "Thanks. I'm glad to…help." She stared at father and son and noticed more similarities between the two, including their names. "Bill and Will? Are you both William?"

"I'm William Drake Addison the third." Bill motioned to his son. "He's the fourth. I didn't want to upset Starr when all the girls called and asked for him, so we used different names."

"Dad," Will said in a cautious tone, playing the role of slightly embarrassed son well. "I'm sure Kelsey doesn't want to hear this."

"Don't worry, son. I won't start reminiscing about your childhood. Not yet, anyway."

Kelsey laughed. Will and his father were lucky. She and her brother shared that kind of relationship, but the one between her and her parents was still strained. Years hadn't erased the painful tug-of-war custody battle they'd put her and her brother through even after the divorce was final.

Will blew out a puff of air. "Just don't pull out the photo albums, okay?"

Bill laughed, deepening the lines on his face. The lines only added to his attractiveness. *Like father, like son.* "You'd better get inside before I get in trouble for keeping you out in the cold too long."

Will's forehead creased. "How is Mom feeling this morning?"

"Good. She's feeling very good." Bill's eyes softened to match his voice. "She slept well last night."

"Great." Will's megawatt smile could melt the snow and chase away the most bitter cold. "Let's not keep her waiting."

"She's in the living room."

After hanging up their jackets in the entryway, the two men led Kelsey into the living room. The mission-style furnishings fit perfectly with the craftsman architecture of the house. Wood paneling covered the walls, and beams lined the ceiling. Sunlight flowed in from the windows and illuminated the room. The natural light helped the greener-than-green plants thrive, and the windows also provided a stunning view of Lake Tahoe. A crackling fire in the river-rock fireplace warmed the inviting room and completed the picture. Well, almost.

Next to the fireplace sat Starr, looking as lovely as ever. Perhaps there was more gray in her brown hair and the hairstyle she wore was simpler than the more product-heavy style she used to wear. Otherwise, she didn't look any different except for the wheelchair. Though Kelsey knew outward appearances didn't indicate the severity the stroke had had on her health. Sometimes, the unseen consequences could be the worst.

As soon as Starr saw her, she smiled. Upon closer inspection, Kelsey noticed the slight droop on one side of Starr's mouth and the way her right hand curled as if keeping a treasure hidden from sight.

Will headed to his mother and kissed her cheek. "Miss me?"

She caressed his cheek with her left hand. "Always."

Will smiled. "Kelsey agreed to help with the wedding."

"Kelsey," Starr said her name slowly with only a slight slur. "Thank you for coming."

She pronounced each word carefully, as if speaking took effort and energy. An enormous amount of relief washed over Kelsey. She smiled with relief at the sound of Starr's voice. She was thankful Starr still had the ability to communicate, unlike her grandmother, who'd found it hard, if not impossible, to communicate. Aphasia, the doctor had called it.

Kelsey pushed the memory aside. It was too late for her grandmother, but Starr… "I hear we have a wedding to put on."

Starr nodded. "Faith has finally found 'the one.'"

Not Starr, too. No doubt, the optimism ran in the family. As long as it wasn't contagious.

Kelsey pasted on a smile. "Good for Faith."

"But Valentine's isn't too far away." Concern laced Starr's words.

"Don't worry. Everything will be done in time," Kelsey reassured her.

"Knew I c-c-could count on you."

Kelsey grinned at the vote of confidence and caught Will staring at her, a thoughtful smile on his face. Okay, it was better than a frown, but it was a wasted effort. She refused to be intrigued by him, not again. So, she ignored him, ignored the way her heart beat in triple time, and focused on Starr instead. "Tell me what you have in mind for the wedding."

Excitement glimmered in Starr's green eyes. She

pointed to an alcove off the living room. "My files…"

Bill placed his hand on his wife's shoulder. "Before you girls get wrapped up in wedding talk, we need to eat breakfast, darling."

Love shone in his eyes, and Kelsey realized this couple was truly one of the lucky ones. One of the few who hadn't abandoned the matrimonial ship with most others.

"There's no rush, Mom," Will added. "We have all morning—all day, for that matter. Rome wasn't built in a day, and neither will Faith's wedding. Remember what the doctor said about overdoing it."

Starr started to say something but stopped. Even though she nodded as if she agreed, the light faded from her eyes. Kelsey wasn't sure whether Starr was having trouble articulating or if Will's overprotectiveness upset her. His love for his mother touched Kelsey's heart, but this wasn't the time for him to be overbearing.

Wanting to put the sparkle back in Starr's eyes, Kelsey kneeled next to her and rested her palm on the smooth metal of the wheelchair. "I want to get started, too," Kelsey whispered, "but trust me, waiting an hour or so won't keep us from planning Faith's wedding."

"Not just any w-w-wedding. This isn't like the other four," Starr confided as if it were their secret. "We must give her the wedding of her dreams."

Kelsey wasn't sure what giving Faith the wedding of her dreams entailed. After four completely different weddings, it seemed Faith's idea of a dream wedding kept changing. And now with the fifth… Kelsey's stomach knotted at the thought. "We can do that."

As Starr touched Kelsey's hand, her eyes reflected her gratitude. "That's why we had to have your help. My family wanted to p-p-postpone the wedding, but it must go on. It's important my baby has someone to look out for her and take care of her. I…Bill and I won't be around forever."

"Don't say that."

"But it's true, and if this wedding isn't perfect…"

Starr sounded so defeated. In the three years Kelsey had known her, Starr had never admitted defeat. Not after Faith's four canceled weddings. Not even after a Starr Properties Caribbean resort was demolished by a hurricane. And Starr wouldn't be defeated now, not if Kelsey had anything to say about it.

Tears pooled in Kelsey's eyes. However subtle, there had been changes due to the stroke. Starr was still determined, but her unwavering self-confidence had disappeared.

"It must be p-p-perfect," Starr insisted.

"I promise you, the wedding will be perfect." No matter the effort Kelsey had to put in between now and the wedding day, she would not disappoint Starr. Kelsey would give Faith the wedding of her dreams even if it killed her.

* * *

Today was killing him.

No, Will corrected himself, *she* was killing him. She, as in Kelsey Armstrong Waters. These past few hours at his parents' house had passed slower than being stuck in a plane at O'Hare waiting for a takeoff slot during a thunderstorm.

Why did Kelsey have to be the one making his parents so happy? Mom's recovery and rehabilitation had taken its toll on his parents. Not even visits from Faith or Hope and her kids over the past few months had made them look so relaxed, so like their old selves, as Kelsey had. He knew her ability to set people at ease must come in handy when dealing with stressed clients, but he had to admit that with his parents, her efforts seemed sincere. Will didn't know whether to be concerned or relieved.

And that made him feel guilty because he recognized the changes in his parents. Good changes. Not only had his mother been smiling most of the morning, an improvement over the depression plaguing her since the stroke, but her speech had improved. She still spoke slowly, but talking about the wedding made her pronunciation better, with little to no stuttering.

Will couldn't believe it. And his father…

Over breakfast, Will could visibly see the weight of the last few months lifting gradually off Dad's shoulders as she charmed him with her wit.

Will should have been happy, but he wasn't. The weight Dad shed landed right in his gut and chest, weighing him down. Big time. Mom might be reviewing ideas with Kelsey, but he would be the one working with her, spending all his time with her, living with her. Though, that had been the best option for keeping the wedding a secret. Still, it would be much easier if she left. Not tomorrow. Not after Faith's wedding. But today.

Mom's laughter reached across the room and warmed Will's heart. She hadn't laughed this way in a long time.

Guilt tightened his throat. How could he be thinking of his own comfort when Kelsey was making such a difference for his parents?

"The theme should revolve around hearts since it's Valentine's Day," Mom proclaimed.

Kelsey jotted in a notebook. "Have the colors been chosen?"

"Faith left it up to me."

The pride in his mom's voice made Will smile. For Mom, he would work with Kelsey. No matter how much her presence unsettled him. He could handle two weeks.

"I was thinking red and pink, but that might be too cliched," Mom said. "Besides, my daughter has never been a big fan of pink. Not even as a little girl. What do you think?"

Kelsey tilted her chin. "It's your choice."

"I just…" Mom sighed. "What would you do if it was your wedding, Kelsey?"

Now, this was going to be interesting. Will leaned back on the couch and rested his feet on the coffee table.

Kelsey bit her lip. "My wedding?"

"Yes," Mom said. "What colors would you choose?"

Kelsey crossed her legs and uncrossed them, picked up her notebook, and placed it on her lap.

Will grinned. *Way to make her squirm, Mom.*

"What's wrong, dear?" Mom asked.

He nearly laughed at Kelsey's pained expression. Talk about payback for all her anti-marriage talk. And her kiss in the parking lot.

"I'm used to offering ideas, but I don't want my personal likes and dislikes to get in the way of helping you define what the bride and groom—or, in this case, you—want. You're the client."

"Don't worry about that," Mom said. "You've catered to our whims on the last four weddings. Pretend this time it's yours."

Oh, Mom. You're going to scare her off. Will felt sorry for Kelsey. Well, almost.

"But it's not my…mine," Kelsey explained. "It's Faith's."

Mom smiled. "Humor me."

"Let's see…we had seafoam green and coral at the first, sage and gold at the second, black and white at the third, and cerulean blue and silver at the fourth," Kelsey said.

"Forget about the other weddings. What would *you* do for this one?"

A minute passed. Kelsey's eyes darkened as if she were contemplating the solution to world hunger, not what colors to use in a wedding. "I suppose I'd use intense colors. Red and purple."

"Oh, yes! Faith loves purple." Mom's excitement was almost contagious if one could get excited about colors. "It'll be stunning."

"Stunning," Will echoed, though not as enthusiastically as Mom. His comment earned him a glare from Kelsey.

Mom laughed. "Now, was that so hard?"

Kelsey smiled, and Will noticed she didn't answer the question. "I'll meet with the florist to discuss the arrangements. Do you have any ideas for flowers?"

Mom nodded. "Please get the folder next to the computer, Will."

Mom's words came slower this time and took effort again. As Will headed toward the desk, he glanced at the grandfather clock on the far wall. They'd been working for almost three hours. "We should call it a day."

"Not yet," Mom said.

Will handed the file to Kelsey and sat in a chair next to his father. The two women seemed to be in a world all their own. Every few minutes, he'd catch a word or two. Engraved frames…a string quartet…"Canon in D," a DJ, and flowers.

What was it with women and flowers? Red spray roses, purple violets, grape hyacinths, jasmine, pansies, Laurustinus, Syngonium foliage. It was all Greek, or in this case, Latin to him. Enough was enough. Time to call it quits.

"Mom's been going all morning long. Don't you think we should let her relax and take a nap?" he asked Dad.

"She's enjoying herself." Dad smiled at the pair of women huddled over a spiral notebook and stacks of file folders. "Let's not ruin it."

"But the doctor said—"

"A smile on your mother's face is the best medicine," Dad said. "Trust me."

Will wasn't so certain. Sure, she looked happy, but what about the dark circles under her eyes? Being that tired couldn't be good for her. As he watched her, his jaw tensed. Mom was still beautiful, but she'd lost the spark in her eyes. The vitality that used to radiate from her was gone. She'd faded from a vibrant color into a pastel. His chest tightened.

"That should do it for now." Kelsey closed her notebook. "We've got enough to get started."

"If you have any questions, give me a call." Mom patted Kelsey's hand. "And don't forget to keep in mind what I said about the other…thing."

Kelsey grinned. "I won't."

The edges of Mom's mouth turned up slightly. Even tired, she still managed a smile. "It'll save us so much time when we plan the next wedding."

"Next wedding?" Will stared at his mother, then at Kelsey, who merely shrugged. "What are you talking about? Faith won't be getting married again."

"She won't." Mischief glimmered in Mom's tired eyes. "But you will."

* * *

What had he done to deserve this? He'd been a dutiful son, a loyal brother, a faithful husband, and a loving uncle. But he wasn't getting married again. No way. No how.

Not even for his mother.

Will leaned against the counter in his parents' kitchen, feeling as though he was nothing more than a puppet. As Dad gave Kelsey a tour of the upstairs, Mom sat across from Will with a white envelope on her lap and a strange smile on her face. Maybe this was all a big joke to her. Then again…

"What's this all about, Mom?"

"I hope your father doesn't take Kelsey into the exercise room. It's a mess from my physical therapy."

"Kelsey won't mind."

Mom's eyes gleamed with interest. "She's very attractive."

Will wasn't about to go there. He groaned. "I'm

not getting married again, so whatever you've got up your sleeve—"

"I want you to read this." She handed him the envelope. "After the stroke, I had one of my nurses help me write everything down in case I didn't have the chance to tell you myself. I've been waiting for the right time, but I don't know if there ever will be one."

The emotion in her voice concerned Will. He'd never seen his mother like this, not even in the hospital. A disturbing thought flashed through his mind, bringing a rush of panic, but Mom couldn't predict when she'd have another stroke, so he pushed it aside. Still, apprehension remained. He ran his fingertip along the seal of the envelope but didn't open it.

Mom took a breath and exhaled slowly. "Please read it."

With a sinking feeling in his stomach, he ripped open the envelope and unfolded the letter.

My dearest son,

I'm writing this from my heart. I hope you will take it that way and not be upset with me. First, let me say, I love your father. I truly believe he is my "one." He's not only my right and left hand. He's my heart. But after my stroke, I realized it wouldn't be fair to him to live the rest of his life alone if I died. I'd want him to have a second chance at love.

His hand trembled. "You can't be serious."

Mom's tired eyes pleaded with him. "Keep reading."

Anything else would be a disservice to the love we've shared all these years, to the values we've lived by and instilled in you and your sisters.

I believe Sara would feel the same way. I loved her as if she were my own daughter, but you both were so young when you married. You were traveling, and she was away at school. And though you loved each other deeply, you couldn't spend more than weekends and school breaks together. It worked then, but fate stepped in before you could have anything more.

Jagged raw feelings sliced through his heart. He held the paper so tightly his fingers crinkled the edge of the letter. "You're wrong, Mom. Sara and I…we had so much together. Our marriage was perfect."

"But Sara's gone." Mom reached out to touch his arm. "Please read the entire letter."

Will didn't want to read more. He wanted to shred the letter into tiny pieces and toss it in the garbage can. He continued reading instead.

It's time for you to put the past behind you. You shouldn't grow old alone, loving a memory, when you can grow old with a loving woman by your side. It's time, Will. You need to find a woman who will be your life partner and help you heal. You deserve a second chance at love. It's what Sara would want.

He felt as if he'd been sucker punched. Mom didn't know what she was saying. He couldn't believe what she'd written. Not after all the things she'd told him growing up. All those stories about true love and happily ever after she'd told him and his sisters. The stories about the Addisons who had come before them and how they had a tradition to follow. To uphold. "Does Dad know you wrote this?"

She gazed at him through lowered lashes. "No. When it's time…"

"Mom—"

"I love you so much, and I want you to be happy."

"You have no idea what would make me happy." Will's tone was harsher than he'd intended, but he couldn't help himself. This was his worst nightmare come true.

Mom smiled. "Thank you."

"For what? I yelled at you." He brushed his hand through his hair. "I'm sorry."

"Don't be sorry." Her eyes twinkled. "You didn't yell; you finally talked to me like a real person, not a fragile piece of crystal about to fall off the shelf."

"Is that what this is about?"

"No," she admitted. "It's about you moving on. You don't have to do it today or tomorrow, but I want you to think about what I wrote."

Will didn't need to think about it. There was nothing left for him to do. "I *have* moved on, Mom."

Moving on, however, didn't include finding a "life partner" and "healing." He was doing fine on his own.

Will folded the letter and jammed the paper into his jacket pocket. His mother was wrong, but this must have been a hard letter for her to compose. "I appreciate your concern. Everything you do reminds me how lucky I am to have a mother who loves her kids as much as you love us."

Chapter Eight

As Will paced the length of his living room, Kelsey thumbed through the preference sheets Faith had filled out over the years. Four different sets for four different weddings to four different grooms. A deck of cards would be easier to make sense of and sort through. *Perhaps with a little help…*

Kelsey glanced up at Will. "It isn't so bad."

He tightened his mouth into a thin, grim line. "Easy for you to say."

Will acted as if someone had stolen a closet full of Manolo Blahnik shoes. Not that Kelsey hadn't felt the same way when she realized what the next fourteen days held for her, and she would need every bit of help Will offered. But first, she had to help him get through whatever had happened with his mother. Kelsey wasn't sure what went on while she'd been with his father, but Will had been stoic and silent since they'd returned to his house.

It had to end.

She couldn't afford any distractions with all the work they had to do, and she needed him to stop moping so she could finally get some help. "Your mom loves you."

He stopped dead in his tracks. "She wants me to find a life partner, but what that really means is she wants me to get married again."

He said the word "married" as if it were the name of a virus with a one hundred percent fatality rate. Kelsey knew the feeling. "She only wants you to be happy."

"I'm happy."

About as happy as a four-year-old asked to be the ring bearer at a wedding, endure the torturous ordeal of standing still, and wear a tuxedo during a nuptial mass. Kelsey smiled.

Will frowned. "This isn't funny."

"Oh, it's very funny. If you could see your face." Crocodile tears running down his cheeks and a pout on those kissable lips were the only things missing to complete the cherubic vision in her head. Will was all man, but if he ever had a son, Kelsey could picture what the boy would look like. Cute wouldn't even begin to describe him. Her heart hitched. "You don't look very happy right now."

"Imagine how you would look if your mother wanted to marry you off A-S-A-P."

"I'd be catatonic." The thought horrified Kelsey, but her mother would never suggest marriage to her.

Mom was too involved in her own life and marital status to care about Kelsey's.

"Exactly."

"But Starr's not trying to marry you off. At least not until after Faith's wedding."

"Still not funny."

"Come on," Kelsey urged in her most conciliatory, soothing voice she used with frantic brides. "She's only looking out for your best interests."

He stared at her as if she'd grown horns and turned green. "My best interests?"

Kelsey nodded. "She wants to see her children—all of her children—settled."

"Settled doesn't have to mean married."

"Maybe not to you. Or me. But it does to your mom. She doesn't want you to be alone."

"I'm not alone. I have Midas. I…" He frowned and shook his head. "Why am I even discussing this? I'm not getting married. I couldn't marry again. My marriage was perfect."

Perfect. Kelsey squirmed in her seat.

"Sara was my life," Will continued. "How do I replace all that?"

You don't. Kelsey knew better than to say that out loud. Neither of them saw marriage in their future, albeit for completely different reasons, but Kelsey felt she owed it to Starr to help her convince him. Or at least not dissuade him. "Try to see it from your mother's point of view. She's trying to get all her ducks in a row, so to speak, in case something happens—"

"Nothing is going to happen to her." The determined set of his chin told Kelsey that wasn't a possibility, not on Will's watch. If only life were so simple and predictable.

"She's tying up loose ends because she feels vulnerable right now." And Kelsey realized Starr wasn't the only one feeling that way. Kelsey's heart went out not only to the mother but to the son, too. "She only wants what's best for you and your sisters."

"What's 'best' can't be defined by our marital status. If you read her letter…"

"What letter?"

A vein in his neck throbbed. "It…It's not important."

Kelsey wasn't sure she believed him, but that wasn't her concern right now. "Listen, your mother's simply getting carried away with Faith's wedding. Once it's over, she'll forget all about your relationship or lack thereof. I see it happen all the time."

"I'm not so sure. She seems serious."

"Time will tell. But right now, I need you to put what's happening with your mom on the back burner and focus on helping me with Faith's wedding."

He cocked a brow. "You reconsidered my offer?"

Kelsey hesitated. Asking for help wasn't easy for her to do, but in this case, it was a necessity. "Yes."

A beat passed, and then he smiled. "Why the change of heart?"

She shrugged. "It's not really a change, per se, but certain things aren't as finalized as I'd hoped."

"My mother said she had everything planned."

"She did." Kelsey used her most tactful voice. "She has everything planned conceptually. Making it happen is something entirely different."

"How much do we need to do?"

Kelsey took a calming breath. "Pretty much everything except the invitations."

Will combed his hand through his hair.

Man, she loved his hair. Kelsey gritted her teeth. No, she didn't.

"Where do we start?" he asked.

"I need to see Faith's dress. Your mother said it's here."

"No one can see it. Faith's orders."

"Fine." Kelsey pursed her lips. "But you can be the one to explain to her why her bridal bouquet clashes with her gown."

"Flowers can't clash with a gown."

Men. Kelsey rolled her eyes. Gorgeous or not, he didn't get it. "Oh, yes, they can."

"How?"

"Where would you like me to start? How different styles and fabrics used in wedding dresses can be overwhelmed by the flowers or vice versa? Or would you rather hear about the various shapes of bouquets and flowers you can use that can make or break a gown? Teardrop, heart, nosegay. Would you like me to go on?"

The dazed look on his face was priceless. He might have acted comfortably in her overtly feminine office and not have too much of a problem helping with wedding plans, but getting down to the details of gowns and flowers seemed to fluster him.

Kelsey chuckled, knowing she was victorious. It was cute seeing him kind of flustered but not backing off. At least not yet. She respected how much he was willing to do for Faith. Not all men, especially brothers, would do this much.

"You can look," he said finally, relenting with a heavy sigh. "The dress is hanging in her room."

Kelsey followed him up the stairs. *Cute butt.* She'd love to see him in a pair of Levi's jeans. No—she balled her fists—she wouldn't.

"Did my mom tell you she wanted Faith to wear her wedding dress this time, but Faith said no?"

"She didn't." Poor Starr. Many mothers of the bride wanted to pass on their gowns to their daughters. Kelsey's own mother had a personal collection of wedding gowns, dresses, and even a suit in every style from traditional to sleekly sophisticated from all of her previous marriages, but luckily, Kelsey would never need one. "Perhaps a granddaughter will want to wear Starr's gown someday."

"That would definitely make my mom happy."

A grin tugged on the corners of Kelsey's mouth. She had to tease him a little. "Or perhaps your bride—"

"Don't say it. Don't even think about it." Will

grimaced. "You don't understand. If my mother got wind of that…"

"She'd have her dress cleaned, pressed, and ready to go."

Will nodded. "She would want you to find the perfect veil to match."

"Shoes, too."

He smiled. "And a coordinating bouquet. You wouldn't want the flowers to overwhelm the gown," he said, repeating her earlier lecture back jokingly.

With a laugh, she nudged his arm.

Will opened the door to Faith's room. Kelsey stepped in and nearly fell over.

She glanced around in surprise—no, shock. Romantic, soft, and fluffy described the room and the furnishings. Three adjectives Kelsey would never have used to describe the fifth-time bride-to-be. Three adjectives that perfectly described Kelsey's room at her father's house. "This is Faith's room?"

Will nodded. "You're pale. Is something wrong?"

Wrong? Everything was wrong. This had to be an anomaly.

Kelsey thought she and Faith couldn't be more opposite. Kelsey was nothing like the fickle starlet. Faith had four ex-fiancés and a current one; Kelsey had never been nor planned on being engaged. Faith was adored by millions; Kelsey preferred to remain in the background. Yet you'd never know there was a difference walking in here.

"This…This could be *my* room. My room when I was growing up."

He glanced around. "I don't picture you in a room like this."

"I didn't picture *Faith* in a room like this." Kelsey ran her fingers over the quilt covering the plush queen-size mattress, she traced the pink and purple wedding-ring pattern with her fingers. Had Faith's grandmother quilted her bedcover, as Kelsey's had? Kelsey's gaze ran up the same four-poster bed as hers, but this one was oak, and hers was cherry. Still… "It's kind of eerie how similar her room is to mine."

His brows furrowed. "Your bedroom is like this?"

She nodded. "My bedroom at my father's house. When he finally convinced a judge to give him visitation rights, he set up rooms for us." She picked up a teddy bear sitting on top of lace throw pillows. "We got to help decorate the rooms when we went to live with him after my mother married husband number two. Otto was allergic to children. Or so he claimed. My brother had to share a room with Samuel, one of our ex-stepbrothers, and later with Jimmy, another one of them, but I had my own room. Cade and I would spend hours in my room. It was our…"

"Your what?"

"Our safe place." Kelsey remembered how walking into her room had made her feel. Safe and secure and whole. "The room has been the one constant in our life. Mom was always moving into whatever new house came with her new husband, but Dad kept everything the same. The room hasn't changed except I have a new stepsister living in my old room now. She's twelve years younger than me."

Kelsey shrugged, hoping she sounded nonchalant, but it hurt knowing when she went "home" she had to stay in the "guest room."

"I can't imagine," Will said.

"Don't even try." Kelsey walked to the vanity table and traced one of the hand-painted roses with her fingertip. "I had one of these. And a chaise like Faith's." As childhood memories washed over Kelsey, she smiled. "Cade and I used them to play therapist."

"Therapist?"

"One of us would be the psychiatrist and sit at the vanity. The other would lie on the chaise and tell the therapist what was wrong. Talking to each other was easier than talking to all the professionals our parents kept taking us to so we'd stay well-adjusted."

"Kelsey, this marriage aversion really runs deep for you, doesn't it?"

Before she could answer, Will touched her shoulder. The small gesture of comfort meant more than it should have, and she ignored the impulse to lean into the touch. Safe and strong and perfect. All things Will was; all things he would never be for her.

A dull ache spread through her, and she shrugged away from his hand.

"It's okay." Kelsey forced a smile. "Lots of people

grow up in dysfunctional families. Present company excluded."

Will smiled. "I never knew functional was the minority."

"You'd be surprised. But I must admit, I envy your childhood. Growing up with parents who loved and respected each other must have been nice."

"Don't forget, childhood is only a small part of our lives. It's who we are now that counts."

"So true." She glanced around the room one last time. Time to be who *she* was. "Where's the dress?"

"Hanging in the closet." Will motioned to the double closet doors. "I'll wait in the hall. Let me know when you're done."

"You don't want to take a peek?"

"And suffer the wrath of Faith? No, thanks." He walked to the doorway. "You might want to prepare yourself."

"Prepare myself?"

"My mother said this gown was different."

How different could it be? Each of Faith's four wedding dresses was different. A beaded mermaid gown for the Under the Sea wedding extravaganza; an empire-waist period gown for the Jane Austen Regency wedding ball; a Vera Wang original for the New Year's Eve black-and-white themed bash, and a silk sarong for the barefoot-on-the-beach soiree. Funny how all her weddings seemed to correspond with whatever movie Faith was making at the time. Speaking of which…

"What is Faith filming right now?"

"It's a high-tech, high-budget alien-from-outer-space movie. She saves the universe from destruction and falls in love during the process." Will stepped into the doorway and turned around so he faced the hallway. "Go ahead and look."

Kelsey wasn't sure she wanted to. Aliens and a Valentine's Day wedding? Laser guns and hearts. Picturing a silver lamé wedding gown, she sighed. That wouldn't quite go with the wedding she and Starr had discussed. *Oh, well.*

Kelsey took a deep breath and opened the closet door. The dress was covered with a piece of muslin. *Hello, sci-fi bride.* She pulled the muslin away and gasped.

"Is it that bad?" Will asked.

"Yes. I mean, no. Not bad. Not at all. Different, yes, but…" Kelsey struggled for the right words to say. "It's breathtaking."

Her pulse raced, and her heart felt as if it had lodged in her throat. Forget about high-tech aliens. Faith had stepped back in time with this gown. Edwardian. That was the era. And Kelsey couldn't believe it. The vintage-style lace gown looked as if it had been made for the veil and wreath she'd been trying on when Will walked into her office.

Talk about a perfect match. What was the word for it—synchronicity. She should have been disappointed Faith would be wearing the ensemble, but Kelsey wasn't. Not when all three pieces looked as if they were made for one another.

Destiny?

Even a realist such as her couldn't ignore fate. Not when it was right under your nose and making you take notice.

Kelsey fought the urge to touch the lace. She didn't want to snag the delicate fabric or smudge it with oil from her fingertips.

What she really wanted to do was try the dress on for herself. Talk about a first. Out of all the gowns she'd seen over the years, not one had ever appealed to her the way this one did. This gown was practically calling her name, begging her to put it on to see how it looked.

Oh, man. Her friends would lose it if they could read her mind right now. She would never live it down. Though, from a designer standpoint, she bet Serena would fall in love with the dress, too. The craftsmanship was incredible.

The scent of roses filled the air. Kelsey glanced around the room. More stuffed animals, a few pictures in pewter frames. But no flowers or potpourri she could see. *Must be a sachet in the closet somewhere.* Kelsey had sachets all over her room. No doubt with all the other similarities, Faith had the same.

Will cleared his throat. "Have you seen enough?"

No. Kelsey blinked. She would never get enough of this dress. Lace covered the entire gown except for a small amount of netting at the neckline. The long sleeves tapered to slight points over the backs of Faith's hands. Intricate flowers had been woven into the lace. Flowers she thought would match those on the wreath. And the flowers for the bouquet…

Kelsey clasped her hands together. She knew exactly what type of bouquet and flowers would go perfectly.

With a sigh, she dropped the muslin back over the dress and closed the closet door. Turning, Kelsey stared at Will's backside. "I've seen enough."

For now, she thought to herself and smiled.

GROUP CHAT #3

Kelsey had ignored all the text notifications, but she finally realized Cade or Christina might need her. Her parents would survive without a reply, but her brother and cousin wouldn't like that. She pulled up her messages. Surprisingly, all of them were from her friends.

Jane: *You can't just mic drop like that! Where are you?*
Elle: *This isn't like you, Kelsey. What's going on?*
Serena: *Proof of life, or I'm calling your mom and your dad.*

Kelsey made sure nothing identifying was nearby and took a selfie. She uploaded it to their chat.

Kelsey: *Here's your proof of life.*
Kelsey: *See? Alive.*
Kelsey: *I'm in the continental US, but that's all I can say right now.*

Kelsey: *And the money was too good to pass up.*

She hoped that appeased them for a bit. But that was all she had time for right now. The clock was ticking, and she had a wedding to plan.

Chapter Nine

February 2

It was too early to get up. Not even Midas was ready to stir at this hour. Will hit the snooze button on his alarm and yawned. He needed more sleep. No, he actually needed to go to sleep. Too bad his mind wouldn't turn off. He wanted to blame his restlessness on his mother's letter, but that had only kept him up half the night. The other half was Kelsey's fault.

Thoughts of her messed with his head. Physical attraction was one thing, but he was drawn to much more than her hair and her smile and her kiss. Spending that time with her last night hadn't been enough. She'd sparked something inside of him, something he hadn't felt in so long. He wanted to spend more time with her, to learn more about her, to peel away the layers until he saw exactly who she was.

But she was his sister's wedding consultant, and if Mom had her way, Kelsey would be his, too. That was why he'd been up tossing and turning all night, torn between trying to push her out of his mind and enjoying having her there before the cycle continued again.

The alarm sounded again.

This time, Will got up. He'd promised to take Kelsey to the inn bright and early this morning. It was early, but forget about it being bright. Not even the sun was up.

Thirty minutes later, they were off. Using a flashlight to light the way, he led Kelsey along the path to the inn. Driving would have been warmer, but it wouldn't have been as fast or as secluded. No matter what, they couldn't let the press see Kelsey. And he could use the walk to clear his head.

Their boots crunched on the layer of new snow. The sound filled the silence of the frosty dawn. Not even a bird was up at this hour.

"We're almost there." Will glanced over his shoulder and aimed his flashlight at Kelsey. He almost didn't recognize her. A wool cap covered her hair. Gloves kept her fingers warm. Her cheeks and nose were pink. She looked young and vulnerable. Protectiveness crept in, but the last person he felt like was her older brother.

"Cold?" he asked.

"A little." She shoved one of her hands into her pocket. "I'll survive."

Survive. That was what he'd been doing every day

since Sara died. Suddenly, surviving didn't seem like enough.

His gaze met hers. Will stood transfixed, watching each cloud of breath rise from Kelsey's mouth, from her lips. He remembered how those lips felt against his. Warm and soft and seductive. Lips made for kissing. Kissing him.

Forget about the freezing temperature outside. He was feeling so warm at the moment he might as well have been in the tropics, not Tahoe. He didn't need his jacket. Or his hat. Or his gloves. He continued to stare.

She glanced at the snow, breaking the invisible bond between them. The silence lengthened between them.

Will needed more sleep to clear the fog in his brain. He hadn't wanted to think about her kiss again. Not when he already couldn't stop thinking about her. She was disrupting his nice, orderly world.

Where were his memories of Sara and her kisses?

He needed to keep his distance from Kelsey. Maybe it would be better if she stayed somewhere else.

"You said the inn isn't much farther," she said finally.

"It's not." He started up the path. "We're almost there."

When they reached the inn, Will concentrated on getting to the service entrance without being seen. Once inside, the heat warmed them. As did the cups of coffee he snagged from the kitchen. He led Kelsey through a pair of double doors and flicked on the lights. The wood parquet floors gleamed. Crisp, white linen tablecloths covered the tables. Each chair was perfectly aligned in front of an elaborately folded linen napkin. Another fine job by the Starr Properties staff.

Will smiled. "What do you think?"

"The room is lovely." She stared at one of the four iron chandeliers hanging from the beamed ceiling. Kelsey's chestnut braid fell back. The tilt of her head emphasized the curve of her neck. A neck that seemed to be asking for nibbles and kisses. But not from him. Definitely not from him. She touched one of the chairbacks. "Have you made alternate dining arrangements for your hotel guests on the day of the event?"

Event, not wedding. She was good, very good. "We have."

She studied the room, including the wood molding and the pictures gracing the walls. She measured every inch with a tape measure.

Will tried not to notice how nicely her well-worn, well-fitting jeans cupped her bottom. He failed. Not a big deal. No crime in looking.

She stood in front of a fireplace so large it could fit multiple people inside it. The height was taller than Will. "Wow, what a huge fireplace. It's beautiful."

Will smiled. "When we were younger, Faith saw these life-size stockings and asked if we could buy them and hang them here for Santa."

"What did your parents say?"

"Yes. Faith was a real cutie and usually got what she wanted. Good thing in this instance. We still have those same stockings, and Santa fills them every year."

"We had so many different stockings that Santa must have gotten confused sometimes." With a faraway look in her eyes, she stared into the fireplace. "Before we left Chicago and moved to Beverly Hills, Cade and I would spend Christmas Eve with one of my parents and Christmas Day with the other. My parents tried to outdo each other with presents. One year there were so many presents we couldn't step into my mother's living room. It was obscene. My dad's house was almost as bad."

"Every kid dreams of a Christmas like that."

Kelsey nodded. "You know what my favorite gift was that year?"

"A stuffed animal or piece of jewelry?"

"A framed picture of my family. My mom, Dad, Cade, and me." Kelsey's smile reached all the way to her eyes. "My grandmother had my mother pick a photograph so she could have it framed, and my mom actually gave her one of the four of us taken before the divorce."

Will not only heard but saw on her face how much one photograph of her family had meant to Kelsey. He tried to imagine what her life was like as a child, pushed and pulled between two parents who didn't love each other. Not only at Christmastime but every day of her life. He couldn't. "Kelsey—"

"This is the perfect setting for the reception, but the ceremony"—she clicked the top of her pen—"we shouldn't have the ceremony here."

Back to business. Just when it was getting interesting again. He wished he knew where her On/Off switch was located. Still, he respected how hard she worked. "Why?"

"If we hold the ceremony elsewhere and Faith cancels, none of the party guests will know a wedding was in the works. They'll think they were only invited to your parents' anniversary celebration. No decorations to remove. No seating to rearrange. No explanations necessary."

"None will be needed," Will said with confidence. "Faith won't cancel."

"You sound so certain."

"If you could see her and Trent together… It's the real thing."

"What about Faith's four other weddings and fiancés?"

"What do you mean?"

"You and your parents are die-hard romantics. What happened to Faith?"

"Nothing happened to her. She got engaged to the wrong men, but now that she's found Trent, everything will work out fine."

The intense look in Kelsey's eyes cut through him and made him feel naked and on display. He didn't like the feeling.

"You honestly believe that?" she asked.

"Heart and soul."

Her eyes were full of questions. She hesitated. "I'd still like to have a backup plan in case Trent turns out not to be 'the one.' We can have the minister renew your parents' vows if the wedding gets canceled. The renewal can take place here, and we'll clean up the wedding ceremony site later."

"Where do you want to hold the ceremony?"

"At your house. What do you think?"

He remembered how she had described the wedding decorations when she first walked into his house. "My mother told you to do what you want. To act as if it's your wedding. Would you like to get married at my house?"

"It's Faith's wedding, and I believe she would like it." Kelsey spoke the words in that cool businesslike manner of hers, but not before he saw the slight quiver of her lower lip.

Not so cool and collected, after all. Another layer to figure out. Will smiled. "Would you like it?"

"This isn't about me."

But it was. Her voice and her eyes told him that. Her hard shell was showing signs of cracking, and Will wanted to be the one to break it apart.

"Would you like it?" he repeated.

"Yes, but it's your house."

Watching the anticipation mount in Kelsey's expressive eyes as she waited for his answer made Will want to take forever to reply. Knowing he was treading in dangerous waters, he should look away, but he couldn't. "We can hold the ceremony at my house."

His reward was a wide grin. A kiss would have been better. But kissing Kelsey was a no-no, as his sister Hope would say to his niece and nephews. A big no-no. As was thinking about her lips, her neck, or anything else. No touching, either. He brushed his hand through his hair.

"Thanks," Kelsey said. "I'm sure Faith will thank you, too."

Chapter Ten

It was nearly midnight. February the second had flown by. She and Will worked in his dining room. The comfortable bed upstairs had Kelsey's name written all over it, but sleep could wait a few hours, especially with the third of the month only a few minutes away. The more she accomplished tonight, the smoother the rest of the planning would go. Besides, ever since she'd snuck into Faith's room two hours ago and stolen another look at her gown, Kelsey had been inspired.

Okay, she was a little tired. She stifled a yawn, but she was inspired, nonetheless. She stood, took her water glass to the kitchen, and placed it in the sink.

Will followed her in there and stretched his arms over his head. "This wedding planning reminds me of cramming for finals."

She smiled. "It's not that bad."

"No, but we deserve a break." He motioned to the coffeemaker on the counter. "Coffee?"

"Sounds good to me." She tucked a stray strand of hair back into her braid. "We might need the caffeine to stay awake."

"Don't tell me we're going to be pulling an all-nighter."

"Okay, I won't tell you."

He groaned. "I'm definitely having a flashback to finals week." As she removed the pot, he plugged in the coffeemaker. "At least it's a pleasant memory of opening one of my care packages."

"Care packages?"

He placed a filter inside the coffeemaker. "My mom always sent care packages during finals week. She filled them with all sorts of goodies to keep me going as I studied and crammed. I can still taste the homemade chocolate chip cookies."

A familiar ache and longing squeezed Kelsey's heart. She turned on the faucet, and water streamed out. "The only thing my parents ever sent were checks to cover tuition and my living expenses."

"At least they paid for your college."

She filled the pot and poured it into the coffeemaker. "Didn't your parents?"

"Yes, but not everyone is as lucky."

Will was more than lucky. He'd been blessed to be born into a family like the Addisons. Not a messed-up family like hers. "You can say that again."

He measured out the dark grounds and dumped them inside the filter. "What do you mean?"

"I shouldn't complain." Guilt raced through her. Her family might not be perfect, but they loved her. Still, the Addison family made her long for things she hadn't wanted since she was a child. "My family could have been worse."

"Now you really have to explain more."

Kelsey replaced the pot. "Your family is *Leave it to Beaver* or *Father Knows Best* come to life. I wish they could adopt me."

As Will turned on the coffeemaker, he laughed. The rich sound was as smooth as warm caramel sauce. "Sorry, two sisters are more than enough. Your brother would be a different story. I always wanted a younger brother."

That was funny. Kelsey chuckled. "Cade doesn't even like to claim any relation to the Armstrongs. He would never cut it as an Addison. Your family is so normal, he'd say you're abnormal."

"We're not that different from other families," Will said.

She rolled her eyes. "Your family is perfect."

"No one is perfect, especially my family."

"Your parents are still together."

"True, but they've had their ups and downs."

"I don't believe it." As she grabbed the sugar container, the scent of freshly brewing coffee filled the air. "What about the Addisons' claim to one love in a lifetime?"

"Even true love hits a bump every now and then."

Will removed two mugs from the cabinet and placed them on the counter. "My parents didn't always get along. I remember one time their yelling woke me up. My sisters, too. We stood at the top of the stairs, listening to the screaming and the shouting. Tears streamed down Faith's cheeks. She stood between Hope and me, holding on to our hands."

Similar memories washed over Kelsey. The fear that she was watching her world fall apart, of having everything she'd come to count on torn away. Her stomach knotted, and bile rose in her throat. "You just described a common occurrence in my house. Cade and I would wake up to the yelling and the screaming. We'd sit together in his closet until we heard the doors slam, and it would be over. For a little while at least."

"The doors never slammed at our house. But that didn't make it any better. Especially that time. My mom broke down crying. I'd never heard her sob like that. She was so exhausted raising me and my sisters, running the Starr B and B, and helping to renovate the inn. But my father couldn't understand why she couldn't give him the attention he wanted. Mom said she didn't have any energy left for him by the end of the day. My father claimed she just didn't love him anymore."

Kelsey knew how much that must have hurt Will and his sisters to hear. Her parents once claimed they'd never loved each other to begin with. Pain gripped her heart, and she slouched against the counter. "What happened?"

"Faith ran down the stairs, begging them not to get a divorce. She always had a flair for the dramatic, even when she was little." Will poured the steaming coffee into the mugs and handed Kelsey one. "My parents were mortified when they realized we had witnessed everything. They had the three of us sit with them in the living room for a long talk about what we'd heard. They apologized and told us not to worry about a divorce and explained how they would work through their problems."

Kelsey had heard that repeatedly from Mom and Dad. Until it became white noise to her and Cade. She added a teaspoon of sugar to her coffee and stirred. "Easier said than done."

"They did exactly what they said they would do."

She held the spoon in midair. "How?"

"My dad took over some of the B and B work, hired a project manager for the inn remodel, and brought home a pizza every Friday night, so my mom didn't have to cook." Coffee in hand, Will leaned against the counter. "They scheduled a weekly date night and would never cancel unless blood, a fever, or a trip to the hospital was involved."

"That's…amazing. It's hard to believe they worked it out." A stab of envy pierced her heart. "If that were my parents, my father would have gone out and found the attention he wanted elsewhere. Who am I kidding?" Kelsey stared into her coffee. "That's what he did. My mother, too. I just wish…"

"What?"

"That my parents could have been more like yours and thought about how their actions affected us." Her hand trembled as she held on to her mug. "They didn't tell us they were getting a divorce. My mom said to pack a bag because we were going on a trip. She stashed us away with a distant Armstrong cousin so my father couldn't find us. She didn't even let us say goodbye to him. My dad was frantic, and my mother loved every minute of it. Things went downhill from there." Kelsey gripped her mug with both hands so she wouldn't drop it. "My parents couldn't work through anything, not even when it came to me and my brother."

"We aren't destined to follow in our parents' footsteps."

"I suppose not, but we can learn from their mistakes." The heat from the mug warmed Kelsey's hands and took away the chill that had taken hold of her. "I've analyzed and overanalyzed what happened to my parents and their subsequent spouses. There's no chance of ever getting it right. I'm certain of that."

"Sure, with that attitude. But, Kelsey, you *can* get it right." The sincerity in his eyes tugged at her heart. *Such a romantic.* "When I married Sara, I didn't expect to have smooth sailing, but I knew no matter what came up, we'd make it. We'd have a couple of kids, a cat, and a dog." Will shrugged. "I got the cat."

"You got more than that."

His faint smile held a touch of sadness. "I know."

"You could try again. Go on a few dates," Kelsey suggested.

"I date," he said quickly. "I'm only human."

"Thanks for clarifying."

He chuckled. "Dating is okay, but in the end the relationships never go anywhere. What Sara and I had…you don't find that every day."

"I'm sure you don't." Kelsey took a sip of her coffee. "You must miss her."

His smile disappeared, and he placed his empty cup on the counter. "I do."

Kelsey couldn't imagine what he'd gone through. From childhood friendship to falling in love to losing the love of his life, all those feelings and emotions were so foreign to her.

She refilled his mug. "So, are you ready to pull an all-nighter?"

* * *

February 3

So much for pulling an all-nighter.

The crick in Will's neck was about to kill him, but that was what he got for falling asleep on the couch. He stretched, only to find his legs tangled in something warm and soft and…

His eyes sprang open.

Kelsey.

She was sound asleep on the opposite end of the couch, legs entwined with his across the large sofa. Her lips curved upward, and Will wondered what dream had put the peaceful smile on her face. Her dark lashes shadowed her fair skin. He wanted to kiss the mole on her cheek.

Right here, right now, all her barriers were down, and he liked that. She wasn't a hardworking wedding consultant. She wasn't the cynical realist who didn't believe in "happily ever afters." She was Sleeping Beauty. All she needed was a kiss to wake her up….

His chest tightened.

He was no Prince Charming. Not even close. Prince Charming wouldn't be watching her sleep like a creep.

But something intrigued him and drove his curiosity. Nothing about Kelsey was surface level. There was more to her cynicism than met the eye. Thanks to their conversation last night, he had a better understanding of why Kelsey felt the way she did about love and marriage. He didn't blame her after everything she and her brother had been through. But Will blamed her parents.

A sigh escaped Kelsey's lips. She shifted, rubbing her calf against his.

A rush of heat raced through him. He allowed himself a minute to enjoy the moment. Lying together this way with Kelsey felt so good, so natural.

His muscles tensed. There was nothing natural

about it. Strange, that was what it was.

Will had been surrounded by women his entire life. His mother, his sisters, his wife. But Kelsey didn't fit into any of the usual categories. Yet he was feeling things he hadn't felt since Sara….

Will untangled his legs and sat up straight.

How could the feelings be the same?

Kelsey was nothing like Sara. Tall and brunette, Kelsey was the antithesis of his petite, blonde wife. But the differences went deeper than the physical.

Gentle, soft-spoken Sara would have been bowled over by tell-it-like-it-is Kelsey. His wife had been easygoing without Kelsey's drive and determination. Sara was the perfect wife; Kelsey didn't believe in marriage. One was milk and apple pie, the other champagne and crème brûlée.

Yet both women made him smile, made him laugh, made him feel a certain something he couldn't quite name. A feeling that wasn't going away even after he'd considered it for a minute or two.

Kelsey blinked open her eyes. "Wh-what happened?"

"Resting our eyes turned into a rest-of-the-night snooze session."

As she sat upright, worry creased her forehead. "We slept here? Together?"

She sounded like a Puritan. Will bit back a chuckle. "If you're worried about your virtue, don't be. We had a chaperone."

Midas slept on the back of the couch. Kelsey looked at him. "What's that noise he's making?"

"That's how he breathes."

"Are you sure?"

"Positive." A memory of a similar conversation brought a smile to Will's face. Maybe Kelsey and Sara had something in common—a concern for Midas.

"You noisy kitty, you." Kelsey kissed Midas's head. "You must do everything your own way, including breathing. But that's okay, handsome."

As she nuzzled her cheek against Midas's fur, a tender warmth wrapped around Will like a blanket.

Kelsey glanced over and saw him staring at her, but she didn't look away. Two lines formed above her nose, and she straightened. "We have an appointment at the bakery. We don't want to be late, and I need a shower."

In the space of a second, Sleeping Beauty had been replaced by Ultimate Wedding Planner. Will shouldn't have been disappointed, but for some strange reason he was. He liked the softer, more playful Kelsey.

Half an hour later, she met him downstairs again. She'd tucked her hair into a wool cap and was wearing a pair of black slacks and a red sweater. She'd put on a pair of round sunglasses and shrugged on a long, oversized black coat he'd borrowed from Hope's closet. "Do you think anyone will recognize me?"

He barely recognized her, especially in the baggy coat. If he remembered correctly, Hope had worn that when she was pregnant with his nephew Connor. He wondered if Kelsey ever thought about having kids despite her stance on marriage. "You're safe."

She smiled. "Are you ready to go?"

No complaints, no yawns. Nothing. Not even a word about sleeping on the couch with him.

No big deal, he figured.

Yeah, right, an inner voice mocked at his disappointment over how quickly she had moved on.

Will ignored it. Ignored the strange feelings clamoring for attention inside him. Ignored how all of this had to do with Kelsey, not Sara.

CHAPTER ELEVEN

Thankful her disguise seemed to be working, Kelsey stood outside the bakery with Will. No one seemed to be paying any attention to them. She probably could have come up with something more clever than a big coat, hat, and sunglasses, but there hadn't been time. She needed to order a wedding cake, and to do that, she needed to taste cake samples. There also wasn't a back door that customers were allowed to use because today was delivery day. Yes, she'd asked Will and even called the shop.

From the street, Fitzpatrick's Baked Goods looked like a quaint bakery, a mom-and-pop shop you might find on any main street in any small town in America.

According to Will, the Fitzpatrick family supplied baked goods to local restaurants, ski resorts, and hotels, including Starr Lake Inn.

The bakery was also gaining a reputation for its cakes—birthday, wedding, you name it. The Fitzpatricks' oldest daughter, Molly, baked cakes that

Will described as sinful. This, Kelsey had to taste. Not only the cake but what Will considered sinful.

Will opened the glass door for her, and a bell jangled. Kelsey entered the bakery. The smell of vanilla, chocolate, and a hint of cinnamon lingered in the air, greeting her like an old friend. Glass display cases held a variety of cakes, pastries, tortes, breads, and cookies. Round tables covered with blue-and-white checkered tablecloths and white wood tole-painted chairs filled the bakery and were crowded with customers dressed in every type of ski attire imaginable. The din of the crowd rose above the morning's ski report being broadcast over speakers placed in the ceiling.

A woman in her early twenties with a fair complexion and copper-colored hair greeted Will with a hug and kiss. Kelsey's stomach flip-flopped at the sight.

Will kept his arm around the woman's shoulders. "Kelsey Armstrong Waters, meet Molly Fitzpatrick."

The woman was the cake baker he'd talked about. Kelsey didn't understand why that made the knot in her stomach loosen. She extended her hand. "Nice to meet you."

As Molly shook her hand, she smiled, a friendly expression full of warmth and enthusiasm. Freckles dotted the bridge of her nose and cheeks. "The pleasure is mine, Ms. Waters."

"Kelsey."

A dimple appeared in Molly's left cheek. "Kelsey, it is. Follow me."

Molly led them to a room with its own door. "Will said you were trying to keep a low profile, so I thought you might want to taste the samples in private."

"Thank you." Inside the room, Kelsey removed her sunglasses. Not only were small plates with cake samples set out next to a pitcher of water and cups, but actual cakes of varying sizes and shapes covered the other tables. Cakes that made Kelsey's mouth water. If they tasted as good as they looked… "I've heard glowing reports about your cakes."

"I've heard the same about your weddings, though Will tells me this one is an anniversary party for his parents."

"Yes, they'll be renewing their vows, and the party will be a wedding reception for them."

Molly's green-eyed gaze met Will's. "How romantic for your parents."

"Isn't it?" he said with his most charming smile. "I hope our visit hasn't caused too much trouble."

Molly batted her eyelashes. "No trouble at all."

Kelsey watched the exchange with interest. She didn't understand why Will's relationship with Molly bothered her. Kelsey thought he was attractive. She had kissed him. She found him easy to talk with, too. But she couldn't allow herself to be interested in him. Wanting to flirt with him or to date him was a bad idea. She had to face facts. The only thing they had in common was planning Faith's wedding. If Molly could look beyond the band of gold on Will's finger, more power to her.

Will headed toward the samples. "Good thing we haven't eaten breakfast yet."

Molly laughed and tapped a binder on the table. "My portfolio is here if you want to see some of the cakes I've made. There are lists of cake, filling, and frosting combinations as well as paper and pencils to keep track of your tasting preferences. I'll be in the kitchen if you have any questions." With that, she left.

"Look at all this cake." Will's eyes were wide as he pulled out a chair for Kelsey and then sat in another. "I don't know where to start."

Kelsey knew exactly where she wanted to start. So what if she was a bit curious? It was only natural, given how closely she was working with Will. "Do you know Molly well?"

"I've known her since she was a little kid." He grabbed a piece of chocolate cake with some sort of red filling.

She glanced at her list. *Must be the raspberry.*

"Hope babysat her," he said.

Kelsey picked up a piece of white chiffon cake with fudge filling. "So the Addisons and Fitzpatricks are old friends?"

"We go way back." He glanced up from his sample of cake. "Why do you ask?"

"I've been to many cake tastings, and this one is a bit…extra. It must have been a lot of work for her to go to so much trouble for you."

"I've had women go to lots of trouble for me, but

Molly isn't one of them." He laughed. "She didn't do all this for me. She did it for you."

"Me?"

"You're the Wedding Consultant to the Stars." Will's laughter relaxed into a smile. "If you like her cakes, you might want to use her again. Why else do you think she agreed to bake a wedding cake on such short notice? She's in high demand around here."

Duh. It was all Kelsey could do not to slap herself in the forehead. She was a professional wedding consultant, not his girlfriend. A jealous one, at that. Kelsey took a deep breath. *Thank you, Will Addison, for turning me into a complete fool.*

He took a bite of a piece of chocolate. "This chocolate fudge is a slam dunk."

"Is that a good thing?"

"It's a very good thing."

"Don't eat it all." Chocolate always made things better. "I want a taste."

He broke off a piece and raised it to her mouth.

She stared into his eyes, unsure for a moment.

"Open up," he said finally. "So you can taste it. This is how wedding cake is meant to be eaten."

As she opened her mouth and he fed her the cake, his fingers brushed her lips. The gesture was so intimate it took her a moment to remember to chew. But when she did… "This is incredible."

"I told you. But wait until you try this one."

She drank two sips of water.

He fed her another piece. "What do you think?"

"Yummy." She took another drink of water, picked up a sample of her own, and took a bite. She penciled a few marks on her preference sheet. "This lemon melts in your mouth."

He sipped from his water glass. "Let me try."

Somehow, her hand remained steady as she brought a piece to his lips and placed it into his mouth.

"This is so delicious." The look in his eyes made her wonder if he was talking about the cake or being fed. She wasn't sure of the difference herself.

"Can I have another taste?" he asked.

Kelsey fed him another bite. He fed her. Back and forth. Again and again and again. They continued to feed each other the samples as if it were the most natural thing in the world. At that moment, it felt natural and right and so many other wonderful things.

She couldn't explain it. She felt so comfortable with Will. Almost too comfortable for knowing him for such a short time. Yet she could talk with him so easily. Open up and tell him things she'd only shared with family. Strange and disconcerting. Not to mention that kiss in the parking lot. Kelsey didn't even want to start thinking about that again.

Will reached over and brushed the edge of her mouth with his fingertip. "You have icing on your face."

"Thanks." The spot where he'd touched her radiated heat. She ignored the urge to touch it, ignored the urge to lick the icing off his finger.

Talk about jumping into the fire. She needed to stand back, way back, or she was going to get burned.

"So, do you have any favorites?" he asked.

Besides you?

She swallowed hard. *Focus. Focus on the task at hand.* "I love the chocolate one."

"Me, too."

"I also liked the lemon."

"Faith doesn't like lemon."

Kelsey felt as if he'd poured the pitcher of ice water on her face. She knew that about Faith. Why hadn't Kelsey remembered? It was her job to remember such details. But with Will around it was easy to forget what her job entailed. Much too easy. She had to be more careful. No flirting, not even a hint of it, and definitely no more kisses. "I forgot."

"The banana is pretty tasty."

"Yes, it is." Kelsey studied the baker's portfolio. The mix of traditional buttercream icing in a variety of styles from flowers made of frosting to real ones. A couple were classic styles but done with ganache that gave the cakes an almost avant-garde feel. A few were the definition of creative with modern styles using fondant that showed her anything was possible. She thought Starr would prefer something less whimsical since the woman seemed to be a traditionalist at heart. Faith had selected different styles for each of her weddings including a bright asymmetrical Dr. Seuss style for her third wedding that didn't happen. So the choices were endless, but if Molly used the different flavors in a tiered cake, that would give everyone choices. And that style would be perfect for the theme Kelsey had in mind. "We could order a three-tier cake. Two chocolate and one banana."

"You know, I liked the lemon, but this isn't my wedding," Will admitted. "But my parents enjoy lemon cake. They order it a lot, which Molly knows, so this would cover our tracks and make it seem like this is truly for their anniversary party. So, I agree on the three-tier cake, but let's sneak in the lemon flavor, too. Faith will never know if she's served a slice of one of the other cakes."

He was something special. Kelsey smiled. "Sounds good to me."

Will ate the final bite of the remaining sample. "Tastes even better."

She stared at his mouth, the corners tipped up in a smile, and remembered the taste of his kiss.

But not as good as you.

Chapter Twelve

February 6

Three days later, Kelsey sat across from Will at his dining room table. Scattered between them were file folders, notebooks, magazines, lists, sketches of the reception room, a phone book, a cell phone, a laptop, and a tablet. The wedding plans were coming together.

"Am I living up to your highly paid, highly qualified staff members?" Will asked.

She hesitated, long enough to make him sweat. "Yes, and I'm even noticing some personal improvement on your part."

"Such as?

"Your eyes aren't glassing over as much," she teased.

"My eyes never glass over." She raised a brow, and he grinned sheepishly. "Maybe once or twice, but for someone who's never planned a wedding before, I'm doing great."

"Wait." She couldn't believe he was a newbie. Not after all he'd done for Faith's wedding. "What about your own wedding?"

"Sara knew what kind of wedding she wanted since she was twelve and took care of everything. I only had to show up in a tux and say, 'I do.'"

"Any regrets?"

"No. It was the wedding Sara wanted."

What did you want? The question sat on the tip of Kelsey's tongue, but she kept her curiosity from getting the best of her. More than once, she'd felt her interest in Will go beyond what she would regularly entertain with clients. Of course, their actions did, too. Kissing in the parking lot. Spending the night together on the couch. Feeding each other wedding cake. None of those things were part of a business relationship. Yet everything had seemed normal, which was even odder. "So, how does it feel?"

Will furrowed a brow. "How does what feel?"

"To finally plan a wedding?"

The edges of his mouth turned up slightly. "It's been...interesting."

Kelsey chuckled. "I suppose 'interesting' is a step above painful."

"I have to admit, the cake tasting has been my favorite so far."

"Mine, too."

Their gazes locked. She remembered staring into his eyes like this as she'd fed him a piece of cake, watching his lips close around her fingers as she pulled them…

Will looked away. "I'm learning a lot, though I don't know when I'll have the chance to use the knowledge again. I do have a greater appreciation for you canceling your vacation and doing all this work for us now."

She didn't know what to say, so she kept quiet.

"Where's the seating chart you've been working on?" he asked.

Kelsey rose, walked to his side of the table, and placed two pieces of paper in front of him. "What do you think?"

As he stared at the charts, Will's scent surrounded her. Woodsy, spicy, and oh-so-male. She felt a little dizzy and grabbed the edge of the table.

He touched her elbow. "You okay?"

"Fine."

"For a second, you seemed to be in another world."

Yes, she realized, *the Land of Good Will Cologne.* She let go of the edge. "I zoned out for a minute."

"You've been working too hard."

"*We've* been working too hard."

He smiled.

She smiled back. "By the way, what's the name of the cologne you wear?"

"Cologne?"

"Is it aftershave?"

"I don't wear any."

"Oh." She gulped, feeling naked and exposed and oh-so-embarrassed. "Cade's birthday is coming up and…"

Will's eyes twinkled with amusement. "His birthday, huh?"

Busted. Heat flooded her already-warm cheeks. *No problem. It could be worse.* She wasn't sure how, but… She cleared her Mojave-dry throat and nodded.

He stared at her, a wry smile on his lips. "Which one am I supposed to look at?"

"Which what?"

"Which seating chart?"

"Both of them."

What was happening to her? Embarrassing herself was one thing, but acting like a total airhead was another. So what if Will smelled good and it wasn't manmade but his own natural scent and maybe a nice bar of soap or even his shampoo? So what if he knew she liked how he smelled, too? No big deal. She could ignore it. Ignore that her new standard of what a man should smell like had just been cemented in her mind and olfactory nerves.

"Why are there two charts?" he asked.

"One is for the wedding reception, and one is for the anniversary party."

Will flashed her a here-we-go-again look and then studied the chart. "This is really detailed."

"No one wants big surprises on the big day, so I

try to be as detailed as possible to see how things will mesh."

"Is that why you were trying on the veil?"

"What veil?"

"At your office." Interest gleamed in Will's gaze. "You say you don't want to be a bride yourself, yet you tried on that veil. Why?"

"I wanted to see if the veil and wreath matched."

"Couldn't you have just held them up together?"

Yes, but she hadn't. Kelsey wasn't sure what had compelled her to try them on. She hadn't felt the need to do that in years, but she wasn't about to admit that to Will. He already knew too much about her. She was a private person, but something made it easy for her to open up to him. Not about this, though. She tilted her chin. "I wanted to see the full effect."

"And did you?"

"I did." She'd seen a whole lot more than that, too. It was as if she'd been transported to another time, another place. Everything she'd never expected to feel—love, happily ever after, magic—had filled her office in that one moment. Her lips trembled with the urge to smile, but she didn't. "Just part of the job."

He studied her, his eyes cool and contemplative. "It always comes back to the job."

"A wedding is serious business to the bride and groom." Very serious. Kelsey couldn't afford to be distracted by foolish romantic notions and Will Addison. Strictly business. That was all their relationship could be, all she wanted it to be. "Wait until you see the schedule I'm putting together. Talk about detailed. Timing will make or break a wedding reception. If it's right, no one will notice, but if it's off, guests know."

"I don't get it." Will raised a brow. "How can you put so much work into a wedding you don't think will last, let alone happen in the first place?"

The way he looked at her made Kelsey feel as if she were disappointing him. Well, he disappointed her because she'd already answered his question the first time he asked it. Either he hadn't listened or her answer hadn't been good enough, which meant he didn't get her. "Look. I agreed to coordinate Faith's wedding, and I'm doing it. What I believe about the situation doesn't matter."

"Situation?" His eyes darkened. "We're talking about two people who love each other and plan to spend the rest of their lives together."

"We're talking about two people who'll be lucky to make it to the 'I do,' so don't start in on happily ever after."

"You are in the wrong business."

"I'm in the perfect business. One I approach logically."

"Love is all about the heart."

"And following your heart will lead straight to divorce court." Or heartache, as in his case with Sara's death.

"Not always."

Kelsey's gaze locked with his. Stalemate.

It was bound to happen. Their beliefs were too different. But that didn't explain the heavy feeling in her stomach. She wasn't going to change his mind or vice versa.

She took a breath and then pointed to the charts. "Tell me what you think."

Will opened his mouth and closed it. A muscle twitched at his jawline, and then he focused on both seating arrangements. "Don't seat Uncle Wayne so close to the bar, and make sure Hope and her kids are near an exit."

Kelsey scribbled a note on the anniversary seating chart. She wouldn't need the other one. "That was too easy."

"Is it usually harder to seat forty-eight people?" He sounded genuinely interested, which was better than his questioning her career choice.

She had to remind herself he might not be the bride and groom, but he was her client, so she needed to be patient and not storm off like a Bridezilla herself. She took a breath and another.

"It can be. Between the bride and groom, their friends, and families, there's a lot to consider." Those words sounded a warning in her head. "Have you mentioned any of our plans to Faith and Trent?"

"No," Will said. "Faith doesn't want to be disturbed during filming. I'm doing exactly what she wants me to do and a good job of it, if I do say so myself."

"What about Trent?"

"If it mattered to him, he'd be the one overseeing the wedding plans instead of me."

Kelsey didn't want to throw shade on Trent, but she was curious. "What does that say about your future brother-in-law?"

"He's a lot smarter than me." Will grinned. "Don't worry. Faith will call if she has any concerns."

He sounded so nonchalant as if they were planning a surprise birthday party, not a wedding. Relaxed was one thing, but this…

What-ifs swirled in Kelsey's head. What if Faith hated the wedding? What if Trent hated it more? What if Faith didn't even show up?

Kelsey took a deep breath. "I wasn't really worried before. A little concerned, but now…"

Will gave her hand a gentle squeeze. "Everything is fine. Faith trusts me. And you."

The only problem was Kelsey didn't trust herself. Not with Will around. And she sure didn't trust Faith.

* * *

"Thank you," Kelsey said to the operator at the San Montico palace. Waiting for her call to be transferred to the royal suite, she shifted the phone to her left ear and lay on her bed. It was only noon, but she was tired.

Kelsey wiggled her toes inside her wool socks to keep her blood flowing. She just needed a little more energy to get through the rest of the day.

She had to admit she missed having her staff there to help her, but Will was doing the best he could for a guy clueless about planning a wedding. At least he had connections and contacts in the Lake Tahoe/Reno area. Between arranging security to transportation for guests from the inn to the ceremony and back to the reception, they had accomplished more than she thought possible this morning. Still, so much work awaited them, work they would do together.

That concerned her. The more time Kelsey spent with Will, the better she got to know him. She liked what she was learning, too. He was a hard worker. He was also devoted to his family. And what a family. Will might say his family wasn't perfect, but they were as perfect a family as she'd ever seen. She enjoyed being with his parents, too, whether it was dinner or only a brief visit to update Starr and Bill on the progress of the wedding plans. With parents like that, Kelsey couldn't blame him for his views on love and marriage and happily ever after, but it was a red flag to her and all she knew to be true.

Forget about how wonderful he smelled or how good a man he appeared to be or how good he made her feel. His beliefs threatened her own. Any temptation to let her heart decide what to do about Will Addison was not allowed, not even for a moment.

She had to forget about his kisses, his kindness, his warmth.

She had to stop thinking of him as anything other than the brother of the bride, the person who was helping her coordinate Faith Starr's wedding.

Bottom line: Kelsey enjoyed his company and appreciated his input. They made a pretty good team. But it didn't—couldn't—go further than that. As soon as the wedding was over…

"Hello?" The familiar voice of her cousin Christina came across the line as if they were in the same room, not a continent and an ocean away. Kelsey smiled. "I hope I didn't wake you, Princess."

"I was just getting ready for bed."

"A little early, don't you think? It's only nine over there."

"I said bed," Christina replied with humor in her voice. "Not sleep."

"Touché. Your message sounded strange." Kelsey traced one of the flowers on the floral-patterned duvet cover with her fingertip. "What's up?"

"Well…"

The way Christina's voice faded worried Kelsey. She sat up. "Is everything okay?"

Silence.

Oh, boy. This could only mean one thing: marital problems. Kelsey scooted off the bed. But that didn't make any sense. Christina and Richard were the perfect couple. Meant—no, destined—to be together. If they couldn't make their marriage work, there was no hope for anyone else. Kelsey paced back and forth until she couldn't take it any longer. "Are you and Richard—"

"We're fine."

Thank goodness. She exhaled the breath she'd been holding. "What's going on, Christina?"

"I wanted to tell you in person, but the press has been sniffing around, and since you aren't coming…"

If it wasn't Christina's marriage, what could it be? Uncle Alan? Aunt Claire? Kelsey was losing her patience. "Tell me. Now."

"You're going to be a godmother."

"A godmother?" Kelsey wet her lips. "I don't understand."

"I'm pregnant," Christina blurted. "With twins."

"Twins?" Excitement mixed with surprise. Feeling a bit dizzy, Kelsey sat. She missed the bed and hit the floor with a thud.

"Are you okay?" Christina asked.

Okay? Kelsey was more than okay. She laughed, and her heart swelled with joy. "I'm fine! Except next time you have good news like that, Princess, make sure I'm sitting down first."

* * *

That evening, Will carried in a box of food Mom had delivered from the inn. As he placed the box on the kitchen counter, he saw an expensive bottle of champagne tucked inside.

Leave it to Mom. "Just great."

Kelsey glanced up from her notebook. Her brows furrowed. "Is something wrong?"

He'd hoped Mom would come to her senses after she'd written the letter. That getting her feelings off her chest would help her see what she wanted wasn't what was best for him. Obviously, she hadn't, and now she was taking things into her own hands. What a joke. Mom didn't know Kelsey as well as he did, otherwise she would never be trying to push them together. Two people couldn't be less suitable for each other than he and Kelsey. Not that he didn't enjoy her company. He did. A lot.

"My mother's trying to play matchmaker."

"Excuse me?"

He pulled out the bottle. Nicely chilled and ready to be opened. Kelsey said he had nothing to worry about. To think, she thought his family was perfect. What a laugh. "Look what came with our dinner."

"Your mother didn't order it, I did."

"You did?"

Kelsey nodded.

Images of an empty bottle of champagne, an uneaten dinner left cooling on the table, and an eager Kelsey sent his temperature rising. Forget about his mother. He had a bigger problem. Himself.

Will cleared his dry throat. "Why champagne?"

"I want to celebrate."

"Celebrate?"

She nodded, motioned to the box, and batted her long, luscious eyelashes. "Care to join me?"

A smile lit up her face. A smile directed straight at him. This could only mean…

Oh, no. Was she planning on propositioning him? He didn't know why else she would have ordered a bottle of bubbly or be acting so…flirty.

Every muscle tightened. Let her down easy. That was all he had to do. And not make a big deal out of it.

Will opened his mouth to speak, but no words would come. He simply stared at her, an odd mix of apprehension and anticipation duking it out inside of him.

She rose from the table and walked toward him. The sway of her hips seemed more noticeable. Her complexion glowed. And her eyes… A million stars had sprung to life in their depths.

A ripple of excitement rushed through him.

She picked up the champagne bottle. "There should be a chocolate cake in there from Molly Fitzpatrick, too."

And oysters for appetizers? He gulped.

He was tempted. More than he should be. But thinking and doing were two totally different things. And what about the wedding they still needed to plan?

If anything happened… Nothing would. Nothing could. She didn't believe in anything he did. Not love or marriage or happily ever after. Not that he was looking for any of those things. He wasn't, and she wasn't, Will realized. Did that mean she was only after one night? His pulse pounded in his throat.

She held the bottle and dried the neck with a towel. Back and forth. Back and forth. Will swallowed. Hard.

"Of course," she said, her voice seductive, "we'll have to wait until we eat this delicious-smelling dinner before we cut into dessert."

His gaze focused on her full lips.

Desire hit him low and hard. Kelsey had flicked on a switch Will hadn't known existed. Forget about cake, he wanted…

"We could eat dessert first." The words slipped out of his mouth. What was he doing? Thinking? Becoming? He brushed his hand through his hair.

Her grin widened. She unwrapped the foil and twisted the wire covering the cork. The bottle opened with a pop, and he thought he was going to pop himself. "I like how you think."

I like how you think, too. And so much more than that.

Trouble, he was in big trouble. *Slow down. Forget she's a woman. Yeah, right.* He'd have to be in a coma.

Maybe this wasn't so bad, after all. He wasn't looking for forever; neither was she.

Kelsey filled the glasses, handed one to him, and raised her own. "To the future members of the de Thierry royal family."

"To…" Will was about to say, "To us." He felt as light-headed as the bubbles rising in the champagne. "What did you say?"

"My cousin Christina is pregnant and asked me to be the babies' godmother."

He blinked, trying to clear his head. She had to mean, "Baby," not—

"Baby's as in possessive or babies as more than one?"

"Twins." Kelsey grinned. "An heir and a spare, according to Christina."

He stared at her, confused.

"But Christina said this is all hush-hush, so please don't tell anyone. NDAs apply both ways in this situation."

His confused gaze bounced from the champagne to Kelsey. "We're celebrating your cousin's pregnancy?"

"Yes. I'm going to throw her a shower. Maybe two. One in San Montico, the other in Chicago. There will be so much to buy. Two of everything, from clothing to toys. I still can't believe she's having twins, and I'm going to be their godmother. That's such a big deal. I'll be Aunt Kelsey. An aunt. I never thought I'd be an aunt. Cade's not planning to get married and have kids. I'll have to knit booties and little caps. I think that's what aunts and godmothers do. But I don't know how to knit. No matter, I'll figure it out."

She stopped rambling and stared at him.

Her cheeks reddened. "Sorry, I didn't mean to go on like that. I'm excited. Was there something else you thought we were celebr—"

"No," he answered quickly as he tried to make sense of it all. This was about babies, not baby-making. It took a moment for the truth to set in and another for the disappointment to wash over him. Kelsey wasn't after him. She wasn't trying to seduce him. Will had only one question on his mind.

Why not?

* * *

What now?

The celebration over Christina's pregnancy had taken a strange turn of events, and Kelsey was confused. Very confused.

Meaningful glances and seductive smiles and an accidental brush of Will's hand that became a tender touch. He couldn't be coming on to her, yet she couldn't explain his actions over dinner earlier. Mind games, overreaction, too much champagne?

Too much bubbly was the obvious answer.

But as she stood at the trailhead across from the inn's service entrance, waiting for Will to return from inside, Kelsey knew it wasn't the champagne. She had only herself to blame for letting him get under her skin.

Will had done nothing to fuel her fantasies but be himself. He couldn't help it if everything he did and said appealed to her on a level she never knew existed.

It had to end.

Kelsey might have told herself to keep it strictly

business, but she must not really have been trying that hard. She needed to put all these fantasies to rest once and for all.

"The coast is clear."

Kelsey jumped at the sound of Will's voice. Talk about having her head in the clouds. She hadn't even seen him approaching.

"You okay?" he asked.

No, she wasn't okay, but she still nodded.

He squeezed her shoulder. "Cold?"

She stared into his eyes. Will's gaze lingered, practically caressing her skin. A slow heat burned its way through her. She'd never felt more feminine, more desirable, in all her life.

Get it over with. Kiss him now so you can start forgetting about him. "N-no."

"Come on, the chef is expecting us."

As she followed Will across the slush-covered pavement, she noticed a few hotel guests. Two of them were men and looked like…

"Reporters," she whispered.

Will turned. Before he could say anything, she wrapped her arms around him. The nearness of him overwhelmed her. Too bad she had to get this over with so she could focus her attention on Faith's wedding.

"Kiss me." Kelsey forced the words from her dry throat and hoped she didn't sound as desperate as she felt. As she raised her lips to meet his, she told herself what to feel—nothing. *One kiss and then…*

Will's lips touched hers. His kiss was as light as a snowflake. Nothing like the mythic-proportion memory that had been making her think too much about his kiss. It was…sweet. Okay, she could deal with this. Nice and pleasant, too. Nothing to write home about. Relief washed over her, and she smiled. Now she could get on with the wedding planning and put all this behind her. Kelsey parted her lips.

Will deepened the kiss, pressing his lips against hers with a hunger that both surprised and flattered her. Kiss after kiss after kiss.

The snowflakes turned into a blizzard. A total whiteout. Kelsey couldn't see; she didn't care. She only wanted to feel Will's warmth, his strength, and soak up the taste of him—champagne and chocolate and something uniquely his own.

Kelsey was caught in an avalanche of sensation, but she wanted to do more than go along for the ride. She leaned into him and met his kiss with a hunger all her own. As he explored her mouth, she did the same with an eagerness so unfamiliar to her. Pleasure pulsated within her, and she quivered.

Will pulled her toward him.

She met him halfway, and his arms tightened around her. So strong, so warm, so right.

Her entire life, she'd longed for permanence and stability and family. She found the promise of all three in Will's arms. Each touch of his hands and his lips shattered everything she'd come to believe over the years.

Happily ever after.

With him.

Maybe it was possible.

He ran his hands down her back, along the curve of her waist, and cupped her bottom. Will pulled her closer, as close as their jackets and clothing allowed. She pressed against him, her body melting against his. She moaned, relishing the feel and texture of him.

Will dragged the kiss to an end but kept his arms around her and his face next to hers. His own breath, ragged and hot, fanned her temple.

"Are they gone?" he whispered.

She tried to steady her uneven breaths. Her heart hammered in her ears. Her lips ached for more kisses. "Who?"

"The reporters."

Her pulse went from supersonic speed to a dead stop. Like a snowball hitting her square in the face and breaking her nose, the reality of what she'd done made her stagger backward. She was in trouble—big trouble.

Focus.

That was what she had to do right now.

She glanced around. "I don't see them."

"That means they didn't see us." He smiled.

Not trusting her voice, she nodded.

"Quick thinking." He slipped his hand around hers, and she nearly gasped. "We'd better keep up the appearance, just in case."

"O-okay." She forced the word out. She'd gotten

more than she bargained for with the second kiss—make that kisses. This kiss was nothing like the first. At least she'd been right about that. Too bad this kiss was better, monumentally better. And now they were walking into the inn hand in hand as if they were a couple. The worst part was, it felt totally natural. Kelsey suppressed a groan.

Somebody just shoot me now. It would be the easiest way out.

CHAPTER THIRTEEN

February 7

The next morning, Will didn't hear Kelsey, so she must still be asleep. He opened a can of food for Midas. As the cat ran as fast as his three legs would carry him, Will dished the food onto a plate and mashed it with a fork.

A kiss. That was all he'd shared with Kelsey—a kiss. Nothing more, nothing less. No reason to beat himself up and lose another night's sleep tossing and turning over a kiss. He'd kissed other women before. He would kiss other women after.

After Kelsey.

A heaviness centered in his chest, squeezed his already-aching heart. Up until now, the only woman who affected his heart was Sara. Up until now…

Maybe he was lonely. Maybe his mother was right about that. Maybe that explained the way he felt. Working too hard, traveling too much, not getting out and socializing enough. As he stared at Midas, his heart overflowed with love for the cat. But something had been missing in Will's life. "It's been me and you for so long, I forgot how nice it is having another person around to talk with. Not that I don't like talking to you, but you don't talk back. Kelsey…"

Midas glanced up from his dish and meowed.

Will rubbed him and fed him a forkful of food. "I like her, too."

Like, he repeated to himself. Nothing more than that. He couldn't go further than that. Unfortunately, that didn't change what was happening between them.

Longing and desire.

Feelings that had lain dormant for so long were springing to life, thawing his frozen heart in the middle of winter. All the feelings had one thing in common. All of them revolved around Kelsey Armstrong Waters.

The out-of-this-world kiss last night he hadn't wanted to end. The way her hand fit so snugly, so perfectly, in his that he hadn't wanted to let go. Even the meeting with the chef had made him feel as if he and Kelsey were the couple getting married, not the pair simply planning the wedding.

The wedding.

Faith's wedding.

Will was beginning to imagine Kelsey as the bride and himself as the groom. It had to stop. Now. The fantasy forming in his mind was replacing memories of his own wedding with Sara.

That was…

Unacceptable.

A silver-dollar-size lump of guilt lodged in his throat. Guilt over having such a good time with Kelsey. Guilt over wanting to kiss her again and again. Guilt over putting Kelsey in Sara's place.

No, Will corrected himself, *where Sara is and always will be.*

Today, tomorrow, always.

Nothing would ever change that. Nothing could.

Yet these feelings for Kelsey aren't going away.

Did it matter?

Not in the long run.

Whatever feelings he might have for her were temporary, like the traffic on a three-day holiday weekend after a good snowfall. Everything on the roads would go back to normal come Tuesday. The same would happen with him.

Will's life would return to normal on February fifteenth. The battle between what he thought was right and what he felt was right would end in a draw. The wedding would be over, and Faith would be a married woman. Kelsey would be long gone, on her way home to Beverly Hills and her dysfunctional family to design weddings and search for unhappy endings.

Not his problem. She was a capable adult. He didn't need to play knight in shining armor to her misguided heart. She would figure out the truth on her own when the time was right. He couldn't do anything about it.

Not even kiss her until she saw the light.

* * *

February 8

Light reflected off the heart-shaped silver frame Kelsey held in the air. She was putting her foot down about this, even if it went against Starr's wishes. "No engraving."

Will rubbed the back of his neck. "It's only a frame."

"First, it's not only a frame." Kelsey placed it on the table. "It's being used as a place card holder at the reception."

"Who cares?"

"I care, and your mother cares."

Kelsey understood why she and Will were edgy. Late nights, little sleep, lots of work. Not to mention her growing attraction for Will. That alone made her skin clammy, her stomach clench, and her heart pound like the bass drum in a marching band. Anxiety attack? Or an ulcer? Maybe Will had succeeded where his sister had failed.

Kelsey pushed her hair behind her ears. "We need to make a decision, or we'll run out of time, and the decision will be made for us."

Will rubbed the stubble on his chin. He hadn't shaved today. Normally, Kelsey only found clean-shaven men attractive, but Will's stubble gave him a rugged, earthly appeal. She wondered if it would tickle if it scraped her skin.

"Buy forty-eight more," he suggested. "You can always return them."

"I don't want the frames engraved. Period. You can't return them if they're engraved."

For the first time in hours, amusement flickered in Will's eyes. The corners of his mouth tipped upward.

"What?" she asked.

"You sound like a bride."

"No, I don't!" The words flew out of her mouth quickly, too quickly.

"Yes, you do." Will edged forward in his chair. "That's why every tiny detail has been discussed to death, and it takes a major peace accord to decide anything. These frames—excuse me, place card holders—are a prime example. You sound exactly like a bride who doesn't want to do what her future mother-in-law wants her to do."

He should know better than to tease her. He knew how she felt about weddings and being a bride herself. Kelsey swallowed around the lump of disappointment in her throat.

"I don't—" The protest died on her lips. Kelsey's jaw dropped. "I do sound like a bride. A *bride*."

Will chuckled. "It's not that bad."

"Oh, yes, it is. It's worse than bad. It's horrendous."

"It's kind of cute."

"It's nothing of the sort." What was happening to her? With her fingertips rubbing her temples, she rose from her chair. "In case you haven't noticed, I'm totally freaked out by this realization."

"I wouldn't say totally." His grin widened. "At least, not yet."

"And I thought you were a nice guy." She paced. "This can't be happening. A bride is the last thing I ever want to be. I'm a wedding consultant. A professional."

"You are a professional."

"I was, but at the moment…" She blew out a puff of air. "I'm supposed to be doing my job, not getting carried away as if I were planning my own wedding." The blood drained from her face, and she stopped. "Do you think I'm turning into a bride wannabe?"

Laughter poured from Will. He wiped the corner of his eye. "Trust me, Kelsey, the last thing you'll ever be is a bride wannabe."

"Thank you." She took a calming breath. Maybe she was just overtired. "I was hoping I hadn't, but I needed to hear someone else say it."

"No problem." He rose, put his hands on her shoulders, and led her back to her chair. "Sit."

Kelsey did, and Will kneaded her shoulders. "You're so tense. Relax for a minute."

His touch made her stiffen. She didn't want his hands on her. What if she really liked it? She was already acting as though this were *her* wedding. Would she start planning the honeymoon next? "Easier said than done."

"Try."

"Okay." Her muscles were tight and knotted, but Will didn't stop. Slowly, ever so slowly, his skillful hands worked magic, loosening the kinks. As he continued the massage, the tension flowed out of her and evaporated. She'd never felt anything like it. She wanted to lay her head down and melt into the dining table.

"Relaxed?" he asked.

"Uh-huh."

"Close your eyes."

They were already closed, but she wasn't about to spoil the moment. He massaged her neck and moved up, his hands in her hair.

"I want you to start over," he said softly. "I want you to tell me about the frames now that you have some distance. Can you do that?"

As long as he kept touching her this way, she could do anything. Kelsey nodded.

"Now," he prompted.

With her eyes still closed, she took a breath. "We need to make a decision about engraving the place card holders."

"Tell me why we shouldn't engrave them."

He was doing amazing things with her scalp and hair. Those hands of his, those remarkable hands. She sighed.

"Tell me why," he repeated.

"If Faith doesn't show up, we can use them for the anniversary party."

He removed his hands. "See?"

She opened her eyes. "See what?"

"You're back."

Kelsey stilled and waited. No errant thoughts came to her head. No emotional reasons for any decision to be made. No sign of bridal anxiety. "Thank you."

"Anytime." He motioned to the silver heart on the table. "So, the frames…"

"If they're engraved, the frames will join the rest of Faith's and her groom du jour's cache of engraved favors—five hundred fishbowls, four hundred bottles of champagne and flutes, three hundred sandcastles, two hundred gold snuff boxes and another two hundred silver tussie-mussies."

"Tussie-mussies?"

"It's from the Regency period, Jane Austen times, and shaped like a cone. Ladies used them to hold their hand-tied flower bouquets at balls. Each flower had a symbolic meaning—"

"More information than I need or want to know."

"You asked." Kelsey, the wedding designer, was back; Kelsey, the overstressed bride, was gone. That wasn't about to happen again. She tilted her chin. "And now I'm asking. You know what I want. You know what your mother wants. You have the deciding vote."

Will sat in his chair across the table from Kelsey. "I abstain."

"Not an option."

His brows drew together in thought. "Engrave the date on the frames and leave off the names."

"I can live with that. Date on frame, no names." Kelsey jotted a note on one of her many lists. She glanced up at Will. "You make a fine mediator."

"It's a necessary skill to develop with two younger sisters." He leaned back in his chair. "Any more decisions we need to make today?"

She checked her list. "No, but we need to work on the favors. We can set up at the end of the table."

"Wait a minute." A lock of hair fell across his forehead, and he brushed it back.

Kelsey wished she could have been the one—no, she didn't.

"Aren't the frames the favors?" he asked.

"No." She opened a manila folder marked with a giant heart to symbolize a favor. Starr had a unique way of labeling her files. "They're the place card holders, remember?"

Will rubbed his eyes. "Why don't we ask Faith and Trent to do us a favor and elope?"

Kelsey did a double take. "I can't believe you said that."

"Neither can I," Will admitted as much to his own

surprise as hers. "Blame it on an overdose of wedding planning. A man can only take so much."

She wadded up a piece of paper and tossed it at his head. Will caught the projectile midair.

"Good catch," she said. "Now, about the favors. We need to decorate and fill heart-shaped boxes with a hand-blown glass heart, chocolate truffles, and a Valentine's card."

"We?"

He sounded as if she'd asked him to wear a pair of tights and a pink tutu. She suppressed a laugh. "It won't be so bad."

"Doesn't that depend on your definition of 'bad'? I didn't even make any of the favors for my own wedding."

She was really looking forward to this. Kelsey grinned. "You're going to have lots of fun with the hot glue gun."

"Hot glue and fun." Will grimaced. "I've never connected the two before."

"Oh, you will." Kelsey winked. "Trust me on this one. You will."

CHAPTER FOURTEEN

February 11

How had this happened?

Three days later, Will stood in his dining room. With the favor-making supplies set up at one end of the dining-room table and the wedding-planning paraphernalia at the other, this was the epitome of a guy's worst nightmare. And he was living it—twenty-four seven.

An hour of using a hot glue gun and fumbling with ribbons and bows and heart-shaped boxes was all he could take. He had only so much patience. And his hands were too big. So they compromised. Kelsey would work on the favors by herself, and he would run the errands and make the phone calls.

A meow sounded. Midas sat on the back of a chair, staring out a window into the backyard.

Will walked toward him. "What do you see, boy? A bird?"

Another meow.

He glanced out the window to see what had captured Midas's attention. Kelsey stood with her head tilted back, catching snowflakes on her tongue. She hadn't worn a hat, so her long hair swung about her back. He loved her hair, especially when she wore it down.

"Meow is right." Will patted Midas's head and watched Kelsey. She looked so happy and carefree as she played out in the snow. Her smile showed how much she was enjoying herself. "Be right back."

Will pulled on his jacket and stepped outside. The scent of pine and tree sap hung in the chilly air, reminding him of Christmastime and chopping down the family tree, as they did every year. "Did you get tired of making favors?"

She glanced at him. "When the snow started falling, I decided to take a break."

"All the errands and calls are done."

"Good for you." She spread her arms out and twirled. With all her hair and a lavender scarf for wings, she looked like a snow fairy. "I'm not even close to being done."

"You don't sound too worried."

"It'll get done."

She sounded so unlike her normally organized, on-top-of-everything self. "Are you okay?"

"I'm better than okay. I'm in heaven. Look at all of this. I've never seen so many trees. You can taste the green. And those mountains. Have you ever seen anything so stunning as those snowcapped peaks? And this snow." Kelsey picked up a handful of powder and tossed it in the air above her. Her laughter bubbled over and surrounded his heart. "It's so fresh and white. You can almost smell it. I never realized that before."

Her enthusiasm was contagious. Will grinned. "You need to get out of LA if a simple snowfall has this effect."

"You may be right." She smiled. "But it brings back so many memories. I used to love playing in the snow. Cade and I would stay outdoors until we couldn't stand the cold any longer. We'd have snowball fights, make snowmen and snow angels, you name it. You must have loved growing up here."

"I did."

As the tip of her tongue darted out and caught another snowflake, Will watched, captivated. He had to get a grip. Nothing had changed between them; nothing was going to change between them. A few more days and she would be out of his life. The prospect didn't seem as appealing as it once had.

She spun around again. "All of this in your own backyard… Tell me what it was like to be a kid here—the skiing, the sledding—it had to be incredible."

"It was great. And not only in the wintertime. We played out here year-round." He walked toward a patch of trees. The snow wet the cuffs of his pants. "Didn't matter the weather or the season. My mother just dressed us accordingly. She was an expert at getting us out the door with minimal hassle. My sisters and I used to have huge snowball fights in the winter and water fights in the summer." He motioned to a clearing beyond the trees. "That was Yankee Stadium, Wimbledon, and Hollywood all rolled into one."

"Active imaginations."

Smiling, he nodded. "It was better than watching TV all day, but we ended up with more than our fair share of bumps, bruises, and broken appendages."

"You and your sisters?"

"Me and Hope," he admitted. "The only thing that ever happened to Faith was a dog bite from a guest's pet. You can still see the scar if you know where to look."

"Your poor mother." A snowflake landed on Kelsey's nose, and she brushed it off. "She must have had her hands full with the bumps and bruises, broken bones, and dog bites."

"Don't forget the blood." Will grinned, remembering his mother's resigned sigh each time something happened to one of them. "There was lots of blood and trips to the emergency room when we were growing up."

"More credit to Starr." Kelsey set out to make a snowman. "Good thing I don't plan on having kids. I wouldn't be able to handle all of that. I get dizzy at the sight of ketchup."

He chuckled. "I'm sure you'll figure it out."

"I won't need to figure it out." She patted a ball of snow together. "I'm better off with no plants, no pets, and no kids."

"You can't be serious."

"I am."

He stared at her like he was seeing her for the first time. Silence stretched between them. "But you were so excited about your cousin's pregnancy. Throwing two showers, buying baby things, knitting booties even though you don't know how to knit. That doesn't sound as if you don't like kids."

"I never said I didn't like kids. I do. I love other people's kids. You can spoil them rotten and give them back," she admitted. "It's too easy to screw them up when they're your own."

His heart squeezed in pain at the thought of her never having a child of her own. "That's too bad because you'd be a wonderful mother."

Kelsey dropped the snowball, and it splattered on the ground. Her startled gaze met his. "Me? A wonderful mother?"

The incredulous tone of her voice brought a smile to his face. Kelsey might not think she was mother material, but she was. "I've seen you with Midas. You've got the touch."

"Midas is a cat."

"Doesn't matter. Even cats need a human mom or dad. And whether you believe it or not, you've got the mothering instinct like my sister Hope had when we were growing up. You'll see what a great mother she turned out to be when she arrives for the wedding with her family."

As he walked toward Kelsey, she took a step back. No matter. Will wasn't about to let her dismiss something so important.

"With all you went through growing up, you wouldn't make the same mistakes as your parents made," he continued. "I know you wouldn't."

"That's so nice of you to say." Gratitude glimmered in Kelsey's eyes and filled him with a comforting warmth. "Thank you."

"You're welcome." One end of her scarf was dragging on the ground. He wrapped it back around her. "So you might not want to be so quick to give up on love and marriage and happily ever after."

She glanced downward. "It won't work."

"What?"

"You can't change my entire belief system with one compliment."

"I'm not trying to." He raised her chin with his fingertip. "What I meant to say was, any kid would be lucky to have you for a mother. It would be a big loss if that didn't happen someday. Emphasis on someday."

He said that as much for his own benefit as hers.

Gazing into her eyes, he felt a sense of completeness, as if a missing gap had suddenly been filled. But of all the women in the world, how could it be this one? One who was so different from—

She blinked. "I wish I could believe…"

"You can." He caressed her cheek, gently tracing a line down to her chin with his fingertip. "Believe, Kelsey. Believe."

She parted her lips, but he didn't give her the chance to speak. He covered her mouth with his own.

So sweet. Melt-in-your-mouth sweet, like cotton candy.

He wasn't sure why he kissed her, but it was the smartest move he'd made all week, right after getting out of the favor-making. But if she kept kissing him this way, he might give the old glue gun another try. And the ribbons.

Her hands splayed across his back, pulling him closer. He went willingly, without a nanosecond of hesitation. He tasted snow and Kelsey and something else, something exotic, a forbidden fruit or magic potion or enchanted elixir. The tastes mingled, blended. Temptation, desire, and romance. He couldn't forget the romance. That was the most important part. He only needed to make Kelsey see it, feel it, believe it.

As she leaned into him, into the kiss, he wound his left hand in her hair. The soft strands sifted through his fingers like silk. Now, this was heaven, and he didn't want it to end.

The snow flurries picked up and circled them. He felt as if they'd stepped into a winter wonderland snow globe. His only wish was that as soon as the imaginary music stopped, someone would wind the key so they could start again. And again. And again.

Will didn't care that everything he'd thought, everything he'd believed, was flying out the door faster than candy on Halloween. He'd care later. He'd bet Starr Properties' newest resort in the Bahamas that he'd care a lot, but not now. Not in this perfect moment.

This wasn't a mere kiss. Kelsey wasn't a mere woman.

He kissed her again and again. She kissed him back again and again. Then she sighed, a quiet-as-a-whisper sigh that spoke volumes. His blood roared through his veins. He was king of the jungle, king of the world. Her lips pressed against his once again. Searching, seeking, finding…

He wanted her. He wanted her more than he'd ever wanted—

Will tore away from her.

Eyes wide and her breathing ragged, she stared at him. A faint blush reddened her cheeks. It wasn't from the cold. Not this time. "I—"

"No, I—"

"I'm sorry."

"I'm the one who's sorry." But the last thing he felt was sorry. "I started it."

She stared into his eyes. "I didn't stop you."

I should have stopped myself. But he couldn't say the words out loud. Because, heaven help him, he hadn't wanted to stop. Not then, not even now. He'd wanted more. All she had to give him.

And it scared Will, downright terrified him. He couldn't remember feeling so out of control with Sara. Maybe he'd forgotten. He'd been carrying memories of her with him for so long. But that didn't make the way he was feeling right.

"Don't beat yourself up over this," Kelsey said. "You didn't do anything wrong."

Will couldn't look her in the eyes. It was as if she could read his mind. How could someone he'd known for such a short time know him so well? It was all so very…strange. Yet, it felt so very right. Almost too right.

She combed her gloved fingers through her tousled and tangled hair. "Chalk it up to the heat of the moment."

"It's freezing out here." Of course, he was sweating. And he wasn't wearing a hat or gloves.

"So it was the chill of the moment. Same difference." She grinned. "I see the beginnings of a smile."

The edges of his mouth curled upward. He couldn't help himself.

She nodded. "Oh, yes. There it is."

"Do you want to talk about…this?"

Kelsey stared at him with disbelief. "Isn't that supposed to be my line?"

"Yes, but you're also the one who should be the die-hard romantic, not me."

"Touché." She went back to work on her

snowman. "There's not much to discuss. We kissed. It's over. And we shouldn't do it again."

"Shouldn't do what again?"

"Kiss."

He might have been thinking the exact same thing, but he hadn't expected her to say it. "You didn't like it?"

"I liked it," she admitted, much to his relief. "But it isn't going anywhere—we aren't, I mean. We're so different. Too different. And the wedding's right around the corner. That has to be the priority. We can't be distracted."

"Do I distract you, Kelsey?"

"Sometimes. But your kisses really distract me." She flipped her hair behind her shoulder. "Do you understand what I'm getting at?"

Will wasn't certain. He wasn't certain about anything right now, which told him exactly what needed to be said. Kelsey was right. "No more kisses."

She nodded. "No more kisses."

Chapter Fifteen

February 12

The next day, Kelsey sat at the kitchen table. Outside the window, glistening snow covered the ground.

She rubbed her tired eyes, fighting yet another yawn. She should be asleep, not daydreaming about kisses and babies and Will. But she was doing exactly that, and she'd done the same last night.

No more kisses.

Yesterday, Will's lips had her standing on the edge of heaven, or maybe the edge of hell. She couldn't be certain which. All she knew was that it had felt good and right and the way it was meant to be between a couple. Self-preservation had her trying to keep herself from careening over the edge. Telling Will they shouldn't kiss again seemed like the easiest way. It would be easier to stop drinking water or even breathing. She touched her trembling lips with a fingertip. She could still taste him, feel his warmth.

You'd be a wonderful mother.

Will had blown her away with his compliment. She never wanted to put any child through what she had gone through growing up, but her aversion to parenthood ran deeper than that. She never planned to marry, and she truly believed with all her heart, a child deserved two parents who loved each other and lived together and were married. Will would probably laugh at her traditional view on family, but she didn't care. That was how she felt, and that was why she would remain single with no kids. The unmarried life had always been what she wanted. The life she enjoyed.

So why was it suddenly not enough? Why did the thought of having a baby suddenly seem so appealing?

Will.

Will and his family of pure romantics.

That was the only explanation. All their happily-ever-after, one-love-in-a-lifetime mumbo-jumbo was messing with her brain. A part of her wanted to believe, but she couldn't close her eyes to the reality of marriage: infidelity, unhappiness, divorce. She'd seen too much to ignore the truth.

Kelsey needed a diversion. Anything would do. She grabbed the Life section of the paper and flipped open the front page. The feel of the newspaper brought back memories of reading the Sunday funnies with her grandfather. Now, she got her news online. Her eyes focused on a headline in the gossip column: "Hollywood's Golden Couple To Split."

Talk about vindication. This was what she needed to reaffirm all she believed and what her heart told her was true. So what if Will's kisses could melt an icicle? That didn't mean squat when it came to marriage. She leaned forward to read the article. "I knew it."

"Knew what?" Will asked.

She glanced up to see him carrying Midas into the kitchen and setting him in front of his food bowl. "Another pair of clients are divorcing. The husband has been romantically linked to one of his co-stars, but his publicist denies any other parties are involved in their breakup."

"That's too bad."

"They didn't have any children, but at least they had a beautiful wedding."

Will shrugged. "You can have the finest wedding ever, but if you don't have a good marriage, the wedding won't count for much except a total waste of time and money."

Her gaze met his. "That wedding wasn't a waste. It was a lovely celebration. A day for the bride and groom to remember for the rest of their lives."

"A wedding and a marriage are two completely different things. One is an event on a given day. The other is alive. It grows and changes and lasts."

"Only in rare cases does it last."

"Do you seriously think any couple wants to remember their wedding once they are no longer married?"

"I…" Kelsey had to think. She'd always believed the wedding and the marriage were separate entities, so the memories would be separate, too. It wouldn't matter if the marriage ended badly. The wedding would still be thought of fondly. And that reminded her. "Yes, my dad is this way. He has fond memories of his and Mom's wedding. He said everyone had a blast."

"So he remembers it more as a party and less of a symbolic union as a couple."

"I suppose." She motioned to the newspaper. "Can I have this article?"

"Go ahead and take it," he said, sounding snippy, but then he half laughed. "It'll be a stellar addition to your divorce book."

Anger surged. She ripped the page out of the paper. "It's a scrapbook, not a divorce book."

"It's sad, that's what it is." He stared at her, an observant gleam in his eyes. "Show business marriages have a higher rate of divorce than other marriages. Bet that validates your unhappily-ever-after belief. Is that why you became the Wedding Consultant to the Stars?"

Her temperature spiked. He'd struck a nerve because they seemed to get along well except for their views on marriage. "I had contacts in the entertainment industry. It just happened."

"You allowed it to happen. With your reputation and skills, you could work anywhere, with anyone. Yet you stay in Tinseltown, catering to divorce-happy celebrities. Talk about a self-fulfilling prophecy."

He was ridiculous. She huffed. "You don't know what you're talking about."

"Yes, I do."

She wanted to respond to the challenge in his voice, but her tongue felt thick in her mouth. Her brain wouldn't function. His words were spinning around in her brain. She couldn't tell her right hand from her left. Nothing made sense. Nothing at all. He was wrong. He had to be wrong. If not…

He was wrong.

Kelsey straightened. "Divorce is a fact of life whether you're in Hollywood or Hoboken. The latest statistics show—"

"Marriage isn't about statistics."

Will sat next to her, plunging her senses even further into chaos while he seemed totally level-headed. He'd showered and smelled amazing. Wait. She was upset with him.

"It's about a man and a woman who want to spend the rest of their lives going to bed and waking up next to one another," he continued.

"Waking up next to the same person every single day of your life?" She shuddered. "Now that's a scary thought."

"Marriage is beyond scary. It's about a love so all-consuming you can't see beyond it. You don't want to see beyond it."

Maybe in his world, not in hers. Love meant misery

and pain. All the things she'd seen her parents go through time and time again. Kelsey shrugged, even though the last thing she felt was indifference. "I can't imagine feeling that way about anyone."

"That's only because you haven't met the right person. Once you do, everything falls into place like the pieces of a jigsaw puzzle. You feel complete. It's like magic."

She'd never felt anything remotely like that. An empty space in her heart ached.

"Look, I'm not trying to upset you, Kelsey. I don't want to argue or goad you, either. But you push my buttons like no one else and…" He blew out a puff of air. "I only want to show you what you're missing out on. What you can't afford to miss out on. Love. It's a wonderful thing."

She realized how lucky Sara was to have found a man like Will, even if they hadn't had long together. Will Addison was one in a million. Kelsey's chest tightened.

"I'll take your word for it." Kelsey worked hard to sound as if she couldn't have cared less. But she cared so much it hurt.

"No, you have to find out for yourself."

His gaze held hers for what seemed like forever. "Find out what?"

"How it feels to share your secrets and your dreams and a piece of yourself with one special person."

Let me share them with you. Kelsey's heart lodged in her throat.

"He's out there waiting for you."

Yeah, right. The only man who remotely interested her was still pining over his late wife. Something which only confirmed everything she believed. Love was one-sided. And no way would she allow herself to end up hurt because he would rather live with Sara's memory for the rest of his life.

***

Will wanted to get to his parents' house ASAP. He cranked up the speed of his wipers to keep his windshield clear of the falling snow and focused on the road. At least the snow wasn't sticking. Dad sounded so excited on the phone. Will couldn't wait to see Mom's progress with the walker for himself.

Part of him felt guilty for leaving Kelsey on her own. But the other part was relieved to get out of the house. Away from anything and everything related to Faith's upcoming wedding. Away from her.

Kelsey.

This morning he'd only said what needed to be said. She hadn't wanted to hear his words, but he owed her the truth. Love was a wonderful thing, and she deserved to know what she was missing. He'd spoken up for her own good. But it turns out, it hadn't been for his own good. Will found that out the hard way.

Kelsey's special someone was out there. Will knew in his heart, and he'd never been so envious of a total stranger. A lucky guy was waiting for her. Thinking about it, about *him,* felt weird and wrong and a whole lot of other things.

But what was he supposed to do about his feelings? His…jealousy?

That was the million-dollar question, and he needed a final answer.

A memory of Sara sprang to mind. His sweet Sara on their wedding day. And another when she brought Midas home with her for summer break. Then another memory surfaced. Only this time, it was Kelsey, the first time he'd seen her in her office. And when she'd picked up Midas for the first time and cuddled him. And yet another of Kelsey kissing him yesterday outside in the snow. Jumbled memories of Sara and Kelsey assaulted him until he could barely see straight, let alone drive.

Will turned into his parents' driveway and stopped.

Sweat beaded on his forehead. He tugged on his shirt collar. The only sounds were the engine and the wiper blades. *Swish-swish. Swish-swish.* Back and forth like the thoughts running through his head. He brushed his hand through his hair.

His memories of Sara remained. All present and accounted for. Kelsey hadn't eclipsed them, but she had carved her own place in the memories in his mind. Now, he was even more confused than before.

CHAPTER SIXTEEN

This shouldn't be happening.

Standing in Faith's room in front of the movie star's mirror, Kelsey blinked, but nothing changed. She hadn't been dreaming. She had really…

"Whatever it is," Christina said on the opposite end of the phone line, "it can't be that bad."

"It's worse than bad." Kelsey gripped the phone. "I—I'm wearing Faith's wedding gown."

Once the words were out, they didn't sound so bad. For about a second. Another look at her reflection and Kelsey bit her lip. Hard.

A loud thud sounded in her ear, and she cringed.

Christina shrieked. "Have you lost your mind?"

"That's one explanation." Kelsey turned to see how the profile of the dress looked. The skirt puddled elegantly at her feet. It would look lovely bustled in the back. On Faith, not her. Kelsey *was* losing her mind. "This must be an ethical violation of the code of conduct for wedding consultants. Not that I've ever heard of such a thing. But I'm sure one exists—"

"Stop. Right this minute." Christina sounded so harried. Must be her pregnancy and all those hormones. Kelsey never should have called her. "Why are you wearing a wedding dress?"

Kelsey wasn't quite sure herself. Blaming it on aliens or ghosts wouldn't cut it. Not with Christina. Kelsey took a deep breath.

"I'm waiting," Christina said.

"Let's see… Will went over to visit his mother. She's been going to rehab to learn to use a walker, and I wanted to put the wreath and veil in Faith's closet so they'd be here when she arrives. And, well, it just sort of happened."

"Putting on a wedding dress does not just happen."

"No, and I wasn't able to fasten all the buttons on the back by myself. That's why most brides need help when they put on their gowns."

"Kelsey. While putting on the dress, you called me. Why and why not just take it off?"

"I can't explain it. All I can say is I was compelled in a way I've never been before. I thought maybe you'd understand. It was like…"

"Magic."

"Yes. No. More like insanity." The minute the urge hit her to try on the dress, she should have packed her bags and gotten out of town, away from all this wedding nonsense, away from Will. He was the real reason she looked as if she'd stepped out of a wedding album from 1910. He'd made her want to feel loved, like a bride. "I uncovered the dress and held up the veil and wreath. It looked so perfect together, I had to see what it would look like on me."

Christina made a noise. "I take it you're not only wearing the dress."

"No." Kelsey adjusted the wreath. "In my defense, can I say the gown and the headpiece look as if they were made for me. And I swear the dress was begging me to put it on."

"A talking wedding dress?" Christina sighed. "Okay, who is this? What have you done with my cousin Kelsey?"

"I didn't mean literally, but it was sort of magical. And I kept smelling roses."

"You caught my bouquet. There were roses in my bouquet."

"That was months ago."

"Maybe there's some leftover magic from the legend of the ring."

Magic would be much easier for Kelsey to buy. "You think?"

"I don't know, but it's strange. Even your voice sounds different."

"I feel different, too." It wasn't only the wedding gown and headpiece she wore, either. Her skin glowed, a radiance not even the best makeup artists could give her. Her cheeks were flushed, not from the cold, not from heat, not even embarrassment for what she'd done. Her eyes were clear and bright and sparkling. If she could bottle this up, add a catchy name, and sell it, she'd be every woman's new best friend.

"What exactly is going on out there?" Concern filled Christina's voice.

"I'm putting together a Valentine's wedding."

"You've planned more weddings than I can count, and you've never tried on a wedding dress before. Who is he? There's got to be a man involved. Tell me his name."

Christina knew Kelsey too well. "Will. His name is Will Addison. He's the brother of the bride."

"Start at the beginning and tell me everything."

Kelsey imagined Christina plopping down on her bed and sitting cross-legged. Would that be uncomfortable in her condition? "You're pregnant and have a lot more to deal with than—"

"Tell me now."

And Kelsey did. She told Christina everything. "I've never met anyone like Will. He's smart, funny, kind, loving, romantic."

"You like him."

"He's a nice guy, but nothing more. And it's a good thing because he's still in love with his late wife. He even wears his wedding ring to this day. He believes his wife was perfect, and they had the perfect marriage." The words tumbled from her lips faster than tears from a flock of bridesmaids during a wedding ceremony. But Kelsey couldn't stop them, didn't want to stop them. It felt so good to get it off her chest and to say the words aloud and remind herself why they were totally unsuited for each other. "Will believes in having one true love and thinks he's already had his chance. He even told me there was someone special waiting for me. Another man, Christina. It's a totally hopeless situation."

"Just because it feels hopeless doesn't mean it actually is," Christina said gently. "Look at Richard and me. He wanted to prove the legend wrong, and I wanted nothing to do with a prince. At first, it seemed like an impossible situation, but everything worked out in the end."

"But that's you." Kelsey removed the headpiece. "A 'happily ever after' has been waiting for you ever since you were a little girl. Remember how Grandfather Armstrong called you princess, and now you are one? Talk about fate."

"Well, he used to call you Tinker Bell."

"Exactly. A girl who hangs out with a boy who never wants to grow up. Need I say more? I'm not like you. I've never wanted nor tried to find Prince Charming. And now that I have…"

"Will is your Prince Charming?"

Kelsey's mouth parted in surprise. "Did I say that?"

"You did."

"I didn't mean it." Whatever she felt about Will had to stop. Maybe when she got back to LA she could throw herself a pity party. Send out invitations, order an obscene amount of chocolate—ice cream, cake, cookies, and candy.

"You can't let this chance pass you by," Christina encouraged. "You have to tell him how you feel."

"How can I do that when I'm not even sure myself?"

"Are you in love with him?"

"Love?" Kelsey's voice cracked. "It can't be love."

Love drove couples to marry. Love brought her parents so much misery and heartache. Love was the one thing she wasn't looking for. A lump formed in Kelsey's throat.

But she didn't know how to describe the new feelings coming to life within her, her heightened senses that made snowflakes come alive, the perpetual smile on her face when she thought about Will.

It couldn't be love.

Could it?

* * *

The wind howled, but Will couldn't see anything outside the window except a blanket of white falling from the sky. No moon, no stars, no trees, no mountains. Only snow. Lots and lots of snow. At least Kelsey would be happy since she seemed to like the white stuff. And with Faith and Trent and Hope due in tomorrow for the rehearsal, Will hoped the storm passed by morning.

Wanting to keep busy, he opened a bottle of merlot and placed it on the coffee table next to a plate of cheese and crackers. With the push of a button, music filled the living room. He added a log to the fireplace and stoked the fire until it blazed.

Above the music, footsteps sounded on the stairs. Kelsey had been upstairs squirreled away, hard at work as usual. He hadn't seen her since returning from his parents' house after dinner.

Will turned away from the window and sucked in a breath. Kelsey stood in the doorway, a shy smile on her lips. She wore her hair down, the way he liked best, and the strands gleamed in the light. Even from this distance, he could smell her perfume.

She took a step toward him. "How'd it go?"

He didn't know how a woman could make a pair of black jeans and a white turtleneck look like high fashion, but Kelsey did. "My mom walked the entire length of the living room."

Kelsey joined him at the window. "That's wonderful."

He nodded. "She told us to hold our applause until she goes up the stairs."

Kelsey smiled. "That sounds like Starr."

"You think so?"

It was Kelsey's turn to nod. "You sound surprised."

He shrugged. This wasn't something he felt comfortable talking about, but with Kelsey…even the uncomfortable seemed easy. "She seems so different now."

"There will be differences, but it could have been a lot worse."

"Still seems pretty bad to me." He stared at the fireplace. Once, his mother had been like those flames. Warm and full of energy. "And…"

Kelsey touched his shoulder. "What?"

"Her risk for another stroke is higher." There, he'd said it, voiced what had been weighing on him since the first stroke. He took a deep breath. "Another stroke could kill her or completely disable her."

"True, but a million other things could happen and do the same thing. To your mother, to you." Kelsey squeezed his shoulder and then let go. "You can't worry about what-ifs. That's not good for your mother or for you."

But the risk was real, too real. "If anything happens to her…"

"Something already did. She had a stroke and survived. Your family has survived, too."

"No, we haven't. We've been floundering like a ship lost at sea without its captain and no rudder. We had to bring in a hired gun to help with the wedding."

Kelsey arched a brow. "I've been called a lot of things in my life, but never a hired gun."

"It was a compliment."

"Thank you." The look in her eyes softened. "Will, not every family can handle a wedding on their own. Lots of people use…hired guns."

"It's not only the wedding." Will wished Kelsey would touch him again. Her touch reassured him, made him feel stronger. "My mom's the one who holds this family together. She always has. Even my dad admits she's the glue. Whenever there's a problem or something needs to be done, my mom's the one to do it or to see that it gets done. And now there's no one."

A thoughtful smile curved Kelsey's mouth. "There's someone. A co-captain, so to speak."

Will furrowed his brows. "Who?"

"You." Her smile widened. "You came to get me. You've worked on Faith's wedding. You made travel arrangements for Hope and her family. You keep tabs on your mother's progress. Make sure your father doesn't get overwhelmed." The warmth in Kelsey's eyes touched Will's heart. "Those are all things your mother would have done, right?"

Her words had such a profound effect on him. He wasn't used to feeling this way and wasn't sure if he liked it. "So, I'm turning into my mom. Just what a guy wants to hear."

Kelsey chuckled. "You're simply stepping up, taking her place for now, like a...pinch runner. I think that's what it's called. I'm not much into spectator sports like football."

He laughed. "It's baseball."

"Same difference." She flipped her hair behind her shoulder. "Two teams, a ball, a score, and lots of commercials."

He smiled. "Thanks."

Her forehead wrinkled. "For what?"

"For making me feel better."

All of a sudden, he was very aware of his surroundings. The crackling fire. A seductive jazz CD playing on the stereo. The wine, cheese, and crackers. The only things missing were candles.

What was he doing?

Will motioned to the coffee table. "I, uh, put out some food in case you were hungry."

Her eyes widened with appreciation. "I'm starving. I skipped lunch and dinner."

"There was a plate for you in the fridge."

"I, um, forgot."

He sat on the couch. "You must have been really busy today."

"I had a few things I needed to do." She sat on the opposite end of the couch. It was better this way, he told himself. "But I failed to get to the most important thing on my list. Maybe food is what I need to fuel my creativity. I've procrastinated way too long."

"You?" He poured the wine into glasses. "I don't believe it."

"Believe it." She took the glass he offered. "The wedding vows have to be ready by tomorrow. Which leaves tonight. It's just…"

"What?"

"Don't you think it's kind of weird to have someone else write the vows? I mean, if you were getting married, wouldn't you want to write your own?"

"Sara wrote ours."

"Forget I said anything."

"This is no big deal. Faith's used to reading lines. This won't be any different for her."

"What about Trent?"

"He's a guy." Will grabbed a cracker from the plate. "Do you really think he wants to write his own?"

"I guess not."

The hushed tone of Kelsey's voice told him she was still concerned. She really was sweet. "Whatever we give them will be more personal than the vows the minister brings, but they can use those if they prefer. No big deal. I'll even help you."

"I'm making more out of this than I should. How difficult can it be?" Kelsey placed her glass on the table and picked up her notebook and pen. "Dearly beloved, we are gathered here again and again and again and again and again."

"To unite Faith and—insert groom's name here—in the state of holy matrimony."

Kelsey laughed. "If anyone—four previous grooms excluded—has any reason why these two should not wed…"

He chuckled. "See, this isn't so hard."

She smiled. "No, but we haven't reached the vows yet."

"We have all night for that."

The lights flickered once. The music stopped playing right on a beautiful high note. Another flicker of the lights, and everything went dark except for the glow from the fireplace.

"The storm must have caused a blackout," Will said.

"I hope the electricity comes back on soon."

"Out here, you never know how long these things will last. Stay where you are. I'll get some candles."

As he walked to the kitchen, Will sighed. Writing wedding vows by candlelight with a woman he wanted to kiss but couldn't. Not exactly how he imagined spending this evening.

But nothing ever seemed to turn out the way he expected.

* * *

Waiting for Will to return, Kelsey settled back against the cushions on the couch and wrapped her hands around her knees. The crackle of the fire, Midas's breathing, and the sounds of the storm more than filled the living room. Sitting in near-darkness was relaxing, and she relished this moment of peace.

Starting tomorrow, the activity would be nonstop until the bride and groom departed on their honeymoon. Two days of putting all her planning and organizational skills to the test. Two days until Faith Starr married Trent Jeffreys. Three days until Kelsey headed home to Los Angeles.

Time was running out. She needed to sort through

and figure out her feelings for Will. The sooner, the better. She wanted to have things resolved, even if only within herself, before she left.

Will returned with two lit candles and placed them on the coffee table. The tapers provided a soft glow—a romantic glow—of light. Combined with the fire, it was the perfect environment for a kiss. Kelsey's mouth went dry.

No more kisses. She and Will had agreed. Kisses would only interfere with what she needed to do. One kiss and she'd be unable to focus on anything except more kisses.

Will tossed another log on the fire. The muscles of his back strained his shirt. She caught herself staring and looked away. This was about staying warm, nothing else. Kelsey readied her pen. If only her mind would ready itself as easily.

He grabbed several pillows from the couch and tossed them onto the rug in front of the fireplace. "Sit closer to the fire. I want you to stay warm."

Candlelight, a crackling fire, a bearskin rug. Okay, it was an Aubusson, not a bearskin. That didn't change the images running through her mind. She kept seeing herself kissing Will, except she was wearing Faith's wedding gown and he was in a black tux. Man, he looked handsome in formal attire. Her dry mouth got drier.

"Come on."

With her notebook clutched to her chest, Kelsey

joined him on the floor. He tucked a quilted throw around her legs. The thoughtful gesture stirred something deep within her. She placed her notebook on her lap but held on to the edges. She was desperate to do something to keep from touching him.

Shadows from the fire danced on his face. "Do you need another blanket?"

"I'm fine."

Or at least she would be once her stomach stopped doing cartwheels and her heart stopped hammering in her ears.

He grabbed another throw from a chair anyway and set it on the floor. "If the electricity stays off, it'll get cold. We may not have any other choice but to sleep down here."

Sleep here together. Not by accident, but by necessity. Her pulse quickened.

Who needed a fire or a blanket to keep warm? She didn't. It was getting downright toasty.

"What about a poem?" he asked.

"Excuse me?"

"We could use lines of a poem as part of the wedding vows. Something romantic, something lasting. Know any good ones?"

Kelsey closed her eyes. She pictured herself standing next to Will at the altar, about to be married. The image was so clear, so vivid. "'Grow old along with me! The best is yet to be…'" The words flowed from her lips.

"That's beautiful."

"Yes." As was the image in her mind. Perfectly wrong. She wasn't the bride. She was a long way from being a bride. Kelsey opened her eyes and saw Will's smiling face. She gulped. Hard.

"I'm impressed you can recite Browning."

"Don't be impressed. I wasn't reciting anything." Heat flooded her cheeks, and she was thankful the light was from the fireplace and candles. "I read the line in a potpourri catalog and must have memorized it for some reason."

"I love how you come up with this stuff." Will laughed, and the rich sound sent shivers of delight down her spine. "Always the cynic, aren't you?"

She didn't want to be a cynic. Not anymore. Something was happening to her. Something Kelsey didn't understand. Tears stung her eyes, and she blinked them away.

"What if we rewrite some of the traditional vows?"

What if they forgot this entire thing? She swallowed around the lump. "You mean, 'I, Faith, take you, Trent, to be my husband. To have and to hold from this day forward'…yadda, yadda, yadda.'"

"Yadda, yadda, yadda?"

Kelsey concentrated on the vows. Losing herself in her work had always been so easy. Maybe too easy. "'For better or for worse, in sickness and in health, for richer, for poorer.'"

"Cherish, promise, pledge, vow," he said.

"Honor, respect, that sort of stuff."

Will grinned. "All the stuff that gives you the willies?"

Forcing a smile, she nodded. "Do you want to start?"

"I'd be honored." He scooted closer to her. Too close for her own good. The space in front of the fireplace wasn't large, but it was big enough for him to keep his distance. "I, Trent, take you, Faith, to be my wife."

"I could have come up with that." Kelsey wrote down the words. "Wait a minute, I already did."

He chuckled. "I'm just warming up. Your turn."

She glanced up from her notebook. "My turn?"

"We're in this together. I come up with a line, then you come up with one."

"Fair enough." As she searched for the right words, Kelsey tapped her pen on the notebook. She glanced over at Will. "Today, in front of our family and friends, I pledge my love and my fidelity."

"That's a good one."

His compliment made her feel all tingly inside. She smiled. "Thank you."

"I promise to be your husband, your lover, and your friend."

His smile, so sincere and open, made Kelsey feel as if he were making those promises to her. She wanted him to make those promises to her. Just as she wanted to make the same promises to him.

Warmth pooled low in her belly. "I vow to be your steadfast partner and to stay by your side in good times and in bad."

"I will honor you, respect you, and cherish you."

The look in his eyes took her breath away. *Breathe*, she reminded herself, but the last thing she needed now was air. She needed Will.

He moved closer, his gaze never leaving hers. "I'll put you and our family first and never let an argument go beyond sunset."

Happily ever after.

She could taste it. She could feel it. She wanted it.

Never mind that "happily ever after" went against everything she'd believed in for most of her life. She couldn't help herself. Not when she could suddenly picture a future with a man by her side, and that man was Will Addison. An image so appealing it made her heart sing. Something so wonderful had to be right.

And that was when it hit her.

Cupid's arrow to her heart.

She loved Will Addison.

Kelsey Armstrong Waters loved William Addison IV.

Loved him with her heart and her soul. "I promise to listen to you, to laugh with you, to love you."

A featherlight brush of Will's hand made her nerve endings dance. His smile softened, and he rested his hand on hers. "And when our time in this world does end, our love will continue on for eternity."

Eternity.

Kelsey's heart sank to her feet. She pulled her hand away and picked up the pen that had slipped from her fingers. Her eyes stung, and she blinked.

Yes, she loved Will, but his belief in one true love, in a love so all-consuming it lasted through eternity, would keep him from ever loving her.

He'd already found his one true love.

And it wasn't her.

CHAPTER SEVENTEEN

February 13

So much for happily ever after.

Only seventeen minutes until the rehearsal was scheduled to begin, and no one had heard from Faith or Trent. Were they or weren't they going to show? Two weeks ago, Kelsey knew where she'd place her money, but she hoped things would turn out differently for the Addison family's sake.

Bill and Starr sat in the living room, holding hands and quietly talking with the minister. Neither looked overly concerned.

In the kitchen, Hope, the matron of honor, looked more tired than anxious, busy feeding a snack to her children. She was everything Will had described and more. Her stylishly short hair, a cap of dark brown curls, accented her natural beauty and didn't require lots of work. With a peaches-and-cream complexion and to-die-for lush, dark lashes, she needed little makeup. Good thing since Hope had almost no time for herself with three young kids hanging all over her. She kept popping into the living room to see what was going on until a "Mommy" cry pulled her back into the kitchen.

Will, however, was another story. As he stood at a window staring out at the driveway, Kelsey caught a glimpse of his profile. His jaw was clenched, his features tight. Her heart went out to him. She wanted to kiss him and hold him and make everything better, but that was the last thing she could do. She glanced at her watch again.

Don't let your family down, Faith.

Don't let me down.

Kelsey would be the first to admit she'd had doubts about Faith showing up from the beginning, but despite what Will thought, Kelsey wanted to be proven wrong. She never thought it would happen—wasn't quite sure how or when it happened—but it had. This wasn't the wedding of Faith's dreams or Starr's for that matter; it was the wedding of Kelsey's dreams. Somewhere between planning Faith's wedding and hiding from the press, Kelsey had planned her own.

And she wasn't going to let Faith screw it up. Forget about having cold feet, second thoughts, or jitters. It was too late for that.

Kelsey wanted to see Faith walk down the staircase wearing the dream wedding dress and the lovely vintage headpiece. She wanted to hear Faith recite the wedding vows she'd written and say, "I do." She wanted to know Faith and Trent would find eternal love and happiness in each other's arms.

Nothing less than happily ever after would do for the couple, even if Kelsey had never believed, never wanted to believe it, until now.

"Here she comes." Relief was thick in Will's voice and sent a wave of it washing over Kelsey.

"Thank you," she muttered.

As Will hurried to the front door, Kelsey followed him. She glanced at her watch. Fifteen minutes to spare. That had to be a good sign.

The door swung open. Clad in a purple cape and matching hat, Faith entered with a flourish. She greeted Will with a hug and turned to Kelsey. "You're looking lovely. The mountain air agrees with you."

Kelsey smiled. "Thanks."

Faith removed her cape and hat and hung them on the coat tree. She brushed her fingers through her long, wavy locks of hair that made women everywhere envious. No hair extensions for Faith Starr. "Where are Mom and Dad?"

"In the living room." Will looked out the front door. "Are Trent and his brother at the inn?"

Faith took Will's hand. "Let's go to the living room."

He exchanged a confused look with Kelsey. All she could do was shrug. Something was going on, but Faith didn't seem overly concerned or upset. She might be an award-winning actor, but no one was that good at remaining calm when it came to their own lives. Maybe Trent was running late.

"Hello, everyone." Faith made her way to Starr and gave her a kiss on the cheek. "You look wonderful, Mom."

"Where's Trent?" Starr asked.

"He's…" Faith wet her full lips; lips one studio executive suggested she insure with Lloyd's of London for seven figures. "He's not coming."

Kelsey never expected the groom to be a no-show. Her heart plummeted to her feet. She sank into the nearest chair she could find as a mix of emotions churned inside her. Anger, sadness, frustration, confusion. She'd always known this was a strong possibility, but she'd hoped, really hoped.

Starr's mouth gaped open. "Not c-c-coming?"

Wrinkles of concern lined Bill's forehead. "The wedding's tomorrow."

Faith took a deep breath. "There isn't going to be a wedding."

Kelsey glanced at Will, who stared speechlessly at her. For the first time in a long time, saying "I told you so" would give her zero pleasure. Tears welled in her eyes.

"What happened?" Starr asked.

"W-we…" Faith's voice faltered.

"You made it." Hope entered the living room, a dish towel in her hands. She dabbed the towel at a wet spot on the front of her heather-gray jumper. The arms and shoulders of her white turtleneck were smudged with chocolate. "Where's Trent?"

The tears glistening in Faith's eyes ran down her cheeks like the spring thaw of the Sierra snowpack.

Hope ran to her sister's side. "What did I say?"

Will wrapped his arms around Faith. "There isn't going to be a wedding."

Hope started to cry, as did Starr. Kelsey watched the exchange of support, hugs, and tears with amazement. Yes, she was the outsider and didn't mean to be unfeeling, but wasn't anyone else interested in knowing why the wedding had been called off?

"What happened with Trent?" Starr asked, to Kelsey's gratitude.

"I found out he wasn't...we weren't..." Faith blinked. "He wasn't the one."

"Come here, sweetheart." Bill hugged her. "It's better to cancel before the wedding, than after. Marriage is too big a step to rush into. You don't want to make a mistake."

"I don't." Faith stared at Starr. "I'm sorry, Mom. I know how much you wanted me to marry Trent, and I tried, but I...couldn't."

"It's okay, honey." Starr's sincerity made Kelsey want to cry. The love between mother and daughter was so strong you could almost touch it. "The most important thing is your happiness."

"That's right. There's someone out there for you."

Hope smiled. "You'll find 'the one,' get married, and live happily ever after."

Bill smoothed Faith's hair. "Your true love is out there. Don't give up."

"Hope and I found ours early," Will added. "You've always been a late bloomer. That's why it's taking you longer."

Found ours.

Kelsey stared at the band of gold on Will's finger. Her heart lodged in her throat.

Faith nodded, but the sadness in her eyes made Kelsey feel sorry for her. Sorry for one of the most beautiful, talented, and sought-after stars in Hollywood. Sorrier than Kelsey felt for herself at the moment. A bad day was one thing, but this…

She wanted to shake some sense into the Addisons. Couldn't they see they weren't helping but enabling? Putting pressure on Faith by telling her Mr. Right was out there waiting for her wasn't what she needed.

No wonder Faith had such a problem getting to the "I do." She had her entire family, all the Addison ancestors, and their history of marrying their "one true love" to live up to. The Addisons' unrealistic expectations of love and marriage were the problem, not Faith. She was only trying not to disappoint her family. No wonder she'd canceled so many weddings.

As her family continued to comfort Faith, Kelsey's anger rose. At the Addisons, at herself. Kelsey's parents' lack of expectations of love and marriage had as negative an effect on her as Faith's family's unrealistic expectations about love and marriage did on their youngest member.

Kelsey couldn't take it any longer. She stood. "Excuse me." All eyes focused on her.

"What is it, Kelsey?" Will asked.

The words were on the tip of her tongue. Words that needed to be said to put an end to this nonsense.

She'd thought the Addison family was perfect, but she was finally seeing the cracks. Or maybe that was just what she wanted to think because the situation was unbelievable. As they coddled Faith, they didn't make her feel any guilt about canceling yet another wedding. They gave her unconditional love and acceptance. And maybe, just maybe, Kelsey was jealous of that.

But no matter what she might think, good or bad, about her clients, her opinion didn't matter. She wasn't a family member; she wasn't even a family friend. She was only the wedding consultant. She'd been hired to plan a wedding, which meant she still had a job to do. "I need to make a few phone calls about tomorrow's...anniversary party."

CHAPTER EIGHTEEN

Staring at her empty but open suitcase, Kelsey sat on her bed with the list she'd made in case she had to pivot to an anniversary party in front of her. She should pack, but she still had work to do. The anniversary party backup plan was officially in effect. The beautiful wedding she and Will had planned and worked so hard to make a reality was now history. The gorgeous dress and veil wouldn't be worn on Valentine's Day.

Disappointment rocketed through her. But a profound sadness made her plop onto the bed and bury her head in her hands.

She'd never felt this way when Faith had canceled her other weddings, or any other bride for that matter. But this wedding had been different. Kelsey had never put so much into designing a wedding before. Her heart and soul had gone into each detail. But it went deeper than that. Much deeper.

Kelsey rubbed the spot over her heart, a spot that ached. How could she have been so foolish?

A knock sounded on her door. "Come in," she called.

Will entered. "How's it going?"

She didn't want to tell him that the backup plan he'd said was unnecessary was making the transition from wedding to anniversary party easier. She also didn't want to tell him how much working with him these past two weeks had meant to her. She definitely didn't want to tell him about the mix of emotions racing through her right now. It might be better not to say much after all since she wouldn't be able to put it all into words. Besides, what good would it do?

Kelsey cleared her tight throat. "Okay."

He noticed her suitcase. "Going somewhere?"

She lifted her chin. "I thought I might move over to the inn now that the wedding is off."

"Why?" The one word seemed to contain about a hundred questions.

She would go with the simplest answer. "The last thing your family needs is to have me hanging around. They need privacy, and it'll be easier for me to oversee the party preparations from there."

Yes, that was the simple answer, but it wasn't the only one. Kelsey needed space from the man in front of her who had turned her heart inside out, making her want to believe in nothing but fairy tales. By moving to the inn, she wouldn't have to be reminded of how much she'd wanted to believe everything he said about love.

The tiny spark his beliefs had ignited was extinguished as soon as she heard Faith was canceling yet another wedding, but she didn't feel good about returning to the world she'd known was true all along. She hadn't wanted Will to be wrong. She didn't want to be near him, where she might have to fight the temptation to try for something more, when her deepest fears were just confirmed by his sister. In the end, Kelsey had been right about Faith and about love.

His brows furrowed. The lines on his forehead deepened. "Are you sure you want to be at the inn?"

"Yes." She wouldn't give him the opportunity to change her mind about moving to the inn. "How is Faith doing?"

"Better." The tightness around his mouth eased. "She'll be okay. There's someone out there for her—"

"Stop it." The words shot out before Kelsey could stop them. Her patience had been worn too thin.

"Stop what?"

"Faith doesn't need to hear about finding her one true love. She just broke up with her fiancé and canceled yet another wedding. Give her some time to catch her breath, not get all pumped up to find Mr. Right."

"There's nothing wrong with telling her—"

"Yes, there is." Kelsey cut Will off. The words she'd wanted to say earlier were ready to spill out of her now. "If you'd left Faith alone and stopped putting so much pressure on her to find 'the one,' she would be married with a couple of kids by now. Can't you see what you and your family are doing to her?"

Will frowned. "We're not doing anything to her."

"You're influencing how she views love and marriage."

He shook his head. "We're trying to help her."

"The best way to help is to let her figure it out on her own. It's her life, not yours or your family's."

Kelsey's words echoed in her mind, taking root in her brain. She replayed them over in her mind as if they were stuck on some kind of loop. Realization hit her with the force of a 7.8 earthquake.

Oh my goodness. She took a breath, forcing air into her lungs. Faith hadn't been the only one in this situation. Kelsey had done the same thing. Her pulse sped up. She'd done the same thing by allowing her parents to influence the way she viewed love and marriage. Different views than the ones Faith had been indoctrinated with, but oh-so-similar outcomes.

I'm wrong.

How had she not seen that before? She had no idea, but seeing Faith with her family today had opened Kelsey's eyes to her own situation.

I'm wrong.

She'd never been so happy to admit that.

Now, it was time for Kelsey to change what she'd been doing and thinking.

I'm wrong.

She'd been mistaken. It was as simple as that.

She was resisting love for all the wrong reasons. Her feelings were new. Of course, there would be uncertainty and doubts. But that didn't mean those feelings were wrong. Life held no guarantees. Why would she assume there would be any with love? She deserved a happy ending as much as the next person. She truly did.

Will rubbed his neck. "We never meant…"

"I know that, and I'm sure Faith knows that, too." Kelsey smiled, feeling something bloom inside her. This wasn't the end but the beginning. The only problem was she didn't know what she wanted to start. "Your sister will find someone to love and marry and live happily ever after with, but let her do it on her own terms at her own pace, without any pressure from any of you."

He did a double take. "Wait. Did I hear you correctly?"

Kelsey nodded. Time to put up or shut up. At this point, she had nothing to lose. "What would you say if…" Her courage faltered.

"What?"

Kelsey had to do this. Now. Whatever Will's reaction, she had to take the chance or live with the regret. She inhaled deeply. "Would you come with me to San Montico?"

"San Montico?"

"I'd like to see my cousin, and I thought it might be nice if you…we…went together. We could see how we get along away from all this wedding planning."

He shifted his weight between his feet. "We don't need to go away to know if we get along. We both know we do."

Her heart filled with hope. She was so happy he saw it, too. "Might be fun."

Will paused. He opened his mouth and then closed it.

Her heart thudded so loudly she wondered if he could hear it. "What?"

"If I say yes and we go away together, you know that's all I could give you. Once we got back, it would be over. Is that enough for you?"

"No." How quickly she answered surprised both of them, but what he'd offered wasn't what she wanted or could accept any longer. "Before you and your family changed my mind about the possibility of true love and happily ever after, I may have considered it, but now…" She stared into his eyes. "Don't you even want to try?"

"There's nothing to try." His tone was flippant.

Kelsey flinched as if she'd been slapped in the face. She half laughed. That was better than crying. "Guess I asked for that one."

"I didn't mean—"

"Yes, you did." Of that, she had no doubt.

As he brushed his hand through his hair, the gold band on his finger gleamed, reflecting the light from the lamp. He still wasn't over Sara.

Nothing Kelsey could do or say would change that. He'd told her in the many times he'd mentioned his late wife. She hadn't thought it would be an issue when she wasn't looking for anything serious, but the truth was Sara's memory had been a protective wall between them, keeping Kelsey safe. Now, his past was a wall keeping them apart. But that was on her for not listening. "It's…okay."

Okay, that he didn't need her. Okay that he didn't want her. Okay that he didn't love her.

This love stuff really hurts.

Just as she found her heart, she lost it in the same instant. No guarantees. Too bad that didn't make her feel any better or hurt any less. But at least she'd taken her shot. What more could she have done?

Nothing. Her eyes stung, and she blinked. No way would she cry in front of him.

"I never meant to hurt you." Regret shone in his eyes. "I do care about you."

Care, not love. She wouldn't settle for anything less than the whole enchilada. And Will couldn't give that to her. Someday, after a few years of therapy, she might find someone who could.

"Say something," he urged. "Please."

She took another breath. "You're a hypocrite."

He drew back. "Excuse me?"

"You wax poetic about how important love is for everyone except yourself. The last thing you want is to find love again and have a happily ever after. You're no different than me, except I was at least honest about my feelings."

He stared at her. "I tried after Sara died. I've dated, but you can't replace perfection."

"You told me that no one is perfect."

He wouldn't meet her eyes. "That's different."

"Why? Because it's safer to view the past with rose-colored glasses?"

His jaw jutted forward. "Don't do this."

"Do what? Tell the truth?"

"We've had fun." He took a step back. "Can't we leave it at that?"

"Looks like we're going to have to, aren't we?"

"I don't want you to hate me."

"I don't hate you. I…" Kelsey almost laughed when she realized she was about to tell him she loved him. Talk about bad timing. "I want to thank you. You and your family opened my mind and my heart to everything I was missing out on before."

"Missing?"

"Happily ever after and all that stuff."

His eyes widened. "Does that include marriage?"

"Only time will tell. Right now, I'm taking tiny baby steps." Those, however, felt like Sasquatch-size strides at the moment. "Though I will admit, I don't and won't ever buy into the 'one love in a lifetime' you Addisons subscribe to."

Thank goodness. Otherwise, she would be spending the rest of her life alone since she was sure Will could never be hers.

He stared at her, an unreadable expression on his face.

"But I can easily live with true love." She flipped her hair behind her shoulder and looked him squarely in the eyes. "I just wonder how you can live without it."

* * *

Don't walk away from her! As he left Kelsey's room, Will ignored the voice crying out in his head. Ignored the way her words had rocked his world. Ignored how walking out of her room felt like one of the stupidest things he'd ever done.

But he had no choice.

"It would never work," he said out loud as he entered the kitchen. "I had my chance."

"Talking to yourself, big brother?" Faith's eyes were red from crying, but the tears no longer flowed. "It must be serious."

"It's nothing."

Faith raised a perfectly arched brow. "Then why do you look as if you've lost your best friend?"

Because I have.

The thought slammed into him with the force of a three-hundred-pound offensive lineman. What was he thinking? Kelsey wasn't his best friend. He hardly knew her.

The last thing he felt was indifference, but he shrugged anyway.

Faith poured him a cup of coffee. "This doesn't have anything to do with Kelsey, does it?"

"Why would you think that?"

"I noticed the glances the two of you exchanged. What's going on?"

"Nothing."

"Your choice or hers?"

"Mine."

"How do you feel about her?"

The emotions nearly overwhelmed him. He didn't, couldn't, say anything.

"You've got it bad." Faith tsked. "Why aren't you doing something about it?"

He hesitated. "Sara."

Faith pursed her lips. "Don't sacrifice a second chance at love for a memory."

"Sara's more than a memory." He looked away. "She was the love of my life. She was my life."

"I know how much you loved Sara. I loved her, too," Faith admitted. "But none of us know what would have happened had she lived."

"What do you mean?"

"Your marriage."

"My marriage was…fine." He couldn't quite bring himself to say perfect.

"Of course, it was. But with all your traveling, Sara being in graduate school, who knows what might have happened when you were finally together in the same place for more than a few weeks at a time?"

"Have you been talking to Mom about this?"

"No."

"I loved Sara. I'll always love her."

"But she's gone, Will." Faith squeezed his shoulder. "Sara wouldn't want you to spend the rest of your life alone."

"I'm not alone."

"You are alone," Faith said sternly. "It's time you took off the blinders and realized it yourself. Go ahead and say goodbye to Kelsey, but at least acknowledge what you're losing."

With that, Faith left the room. Always the drama princess, her flair had paved her way to stardom. But in this instance, she couldn't be more wrong.

Will pulled on his jacket and gloves. He needed to get out of here. Away from everyone and everything for a few minutes. He stepped outside.

The cold stung his lungs, but he wasn't about to turn back. He needed to get his head on straight. He hiked up a path to a scenic view overlooking the lake. A squirrel chattered overhead on a nearby tree branch.

Sara used to love it here. Memories of her and their time together filled his mind. Life with her had been so perfect. And their marriage, a never-ending honeymoon.

A honeymoon.

His mother's letter came back to him. *An extended honeymoon.* That was what she'd called it; that was exactly what it had been. Not only for their two years of marriage but also the four years before when they'd attended different colleges.

His mother was right. Faith, too.

Will raked his hand through his hair. He and Sara loved each other, lived for each other, but their marriage hadn't been real yet. They never had the opportunity to make any of the day-in and day-out compromises necessary for a marriage to succeed.

What he and Kelsey shared planning Faith's wedding was more like a marriage with compromise and give-and-take than anything he and Sara had ever shared.

It had been so easy to cling to the fantasy. To cling to the image of one love of a lifetime. To cling to the notion of what his and Sara's future would have been.

Because it was safe and kept his heart from having to love and lose again.

Loving meant losing. Hurting. Being left behind.

Losing Sara had tilted his world on its axis and spun it around in the opposite direction. He wasn't sure he could survive it again. And that scared him. But something else scared him more.

Will hadn't kept his heart safe. If he wasn't careful, he was going to lose his heart again. And it would be his fault. He headed back to the house.

The safety net surrounding his heart was in tatters. His mother's stroke and her letter had torn it, but Kelsey's words had demolished it.

He had to act fast and show Kelsey he'd made a mistake. He needed her to be a part of his life.

Today, tomorrow, always.

Chapter Nineteen

Gazing out the window, Kelsey caught sight of the sun peeking out from a cloud. No more flakes fell from the sky, but snow covered every inch of the ground, all the tree branches, and the roof of a gazebo. But rather than a winter wonderland, the landscape seemed gray and foreboding, mimicking the way her heart felt.

Arctic air seeped through the pane-glass window. Kelsey shivered. Too bad the cold wasn't the only thing giving her chills. But she didn't want to think about that right now.

Time to pack. It was the only thing Kelsey could think to do besides walk out and leave everything behind. She emptied her clothes from the dresser and piled them on the bed. If she hadn't been so organized, with a backup plan ready to go, she would have had more phone calls to make and more changes to implement. Her mind wouldn't be so focused on Will; her heart wouldn't feel so empty.

But she'd been organized, and in fifteen minutes, she'd turned the storybook wedding she'd planned for Faith and Trent into an elegant anniversary party for Starr and Bill. Kelsey folded her red cashmere sweater, fighting a sob. She put all her energy into the task and pretended the emotions churning inside her weren't so raw, so painful.

But they were, and not so easy to hide.

Will's rejection was like a knife stabbing her heart. The wound seemed to get deeper by the second. Over time, the hurt would heal. The memories would fade. His hold on her heart would disappear.

She *would* survive. The same way she'd survived the breakup of her parents, she would survive a broken heart. Kelsey had a good life, loving family and friends, and a wonderful career. Just because Will didn't want her didn't mean her life was over. The opposite was true. Her life was only beginning.

Kelsey went to place her sweater in her suitcase but found Midas inside, sprawled on his back. She rubbed his belly and then gave him a gentle push. "Sorry, handsome. You can't sleep here."

The cat merely stretched, taking up more room.

"You're such a sweetie." She scratched his neck. Maybe a pet was what she needed. Someone she could simply love, with no baggage to worry about. Someone who would love her back. "I wish I could bring you home with me, but your daddy won't let me."

Daddy.

An image of Will with children came to mind. Kelsey closed her eyes, picturing them and feeling them and hearing them. Will's children. Her children. Their children.

The visual brought up so many emotions her breath caught in her throat. Her heart pounded fiercely. Tears stung her eyes. She gathered Midas into her arms and buried her face against his fur.

What was happening to her? A broken heart was one thing, but this? Talk about a one-hundred-and-eighty-degree shift in what she thought she wanted out of life. A pet was one thing, but children, too? It was as if her previously dormant biological clock wanted to make up for lost time, and Kelsey was torn. Part of her didn't want to waste a single minute, yet the other part wanted to crawl into the closet and lock herself away from the world.

She rubbed her cheek against Midas's head. His jackhammering purr brought a welcome smile to her lips. "I'll miss you, handsome."

"What about me?"

At the sound of Will's voice, Kelsey looked up.

He stood in the doorway of her room. "Are you going to miss me as much as you'll miss my cat?"

"I…" She tightened her hold on Midas and cuddled him closer. "I don't think so."

Will raised a brow. "Oh, really?"

Kelsey nodded. The truth surprised her. She really meant it. He was the one afraid to love again. No matter her pain, she'd given her all in trying a relationship with him. Will was unwilling to take a chance. She would walk away with no regrets. "Midas goes after what he wants. He isn't afraid to ask for love. You've got to respect that in a man."

"Midas is a cat."

"A male cat." She placed Midas on the bed. "Close enough for me."

"We need to talk."

"Talk?" Talking to Will again wasn't something she could handle right now. Her frazzled emotions could only take so much. She folded a pair of jeans and placed them in her suitcase along with the sweater. "There's nothing left to be said."

"There's plenty to discuss."

"You made your feelings—or rather your lack of feelings—clear. It's best if we leave it at that." She folded a white blouse. "If you're worried about me, don't be. I might have wished for a different ending, but I'm not about to sit around mourning the loss of an unrequited love."

"What are you going to do?"

"Go find him."

"Who?"

"Mr. Right." Kelsey dropped the neatly folded shirt back on the bed. "Somewhere in the world is a man who'll want the love I have to give. All I need to do is find him."

"What if he finds you?"

The intensity in Will's eyes made Kelsey swallow hard. "That'll make my job easier."

"You never take the easy way out. Not the way I do."

She glanced up at him. "When have you—"

"Every chance I've gotten." His jaw tightened. "My entire life, I've had things handed to me. This house. My job. Even Sara. Remember when you asked me about planning my wedding?"

Kelsey nodded.

"Not only did I not help plan the wedding, but I wasn't even the one who proposed. Sara made it easy for me. She had our entire life mapped out from the time we met. She made sure we stayed together, and nothing went wrong. I didn't have to do anything except sit back and enjoy the ride. It was so easy with her." He took a step toward Kelsey. "You aren't easy."

"Never claimed to be."

"You've never claimed to be anything other than what you are. I respect that about you. Me, on the other hand…I've been hiding. Hiding from the truth, hiding from my fears."

She stepped back. "You don't have to tell me this."

"Yes, I do." He took a deep breath. "I want another chance."

Her pulse raced so fast she thought her veins might explode. She took a calming breath. And another. "I can't do this."

"Yes, you can." He stared into her eyes, and her

resolve started to melt. Kelsey looked away. "We've both changed," he said.

"But not enough." She picked up a turtleneck and folded it. "Not enough for it to make a difference."

"Give me the chance. Please."

The sincerity of his plea touched her soul. Her heart pounded, but something—no, someone—held her back. Sara. "I won't compete with a ghost. I can't…"

"You won't have to," he said. "I loved Sara. She'll always hold a special place in my heart. But I've been hiding behind that love and this ring." He removed the gold band from his finger and held it up. "I just never realized it until I met you.

"I used Sara and our marriage to keep myself safe, keep my heart safe. After she died, I was afraid. Afraid of loving and losing again. When you asked me if I dated, I didn't tell you that the only women I dated were those who reminded me of Sara. I wanted to replace her, replace what we shared. I thought if I could, things would be okay and easy again. That I could love and pretend I hadn't lost everything when she died. But I failed miserably. You can't replace someone, and you sure can't find perfection. Sara wasn't perfect. Our marriage wasn't perfect, but I couldn't see that. I didn't want to see it." He placed his wedding ring in his pocket. "Until you."

A lump formed in Kelsey's throat. Her knees wobbled. She sank to the bed, and Midas snuggled against her thigh.

Will walked toward her. "Sara's death. My mother's stroke. I can pretend all I want, but it doesn't change the fact you can't control what happens in life."

"Love holds no guarantees, either."

"It doesn't. No matter how hard you try, you can still lose." He stared into Kelsey's eyes. "I don't want to lose you. I can't lose you." Will reached out and caught her hand in his. "We haven't known each other long, but I love you. I tried to fight it. I tried to pretend I didn't. But I do. I love you."

Kelsey sat speechless, her mouth gaping. She never expected to hear those words from Will's lips. She never expected three little words to have such an impact on her. Yet it still wasn't enough. She refused to be another attempt for him to replace the love he'd lost. "Why? Why do you love me?"

The edges of his mouth curled up. "I love the way your eyes light up when something pleases you and how your eyebrows knit together when something doesn't. I love the way you make coffee and the lipstick marks you leave on the mug. I love how you can be cynical yet wildly romantic about weddings at the same time. Want me to go on?"

She nodded.

He chuckled. "I love that you aren't afraid to speak your mind, give an opinion, or tell me I'm wrong even when I'm right. I love how staring into your eyes makes me forget everything, including my own name. I love you, Kelsey. More than I ever thought possible. Enough?"

"For now." She blinked back tears. "Oh, Will. I love you, too."

"Why?" He grinned. "You made me spell it out. Fair is fair."

She laughed. "Let's see…I love how you hand-feed Midas his food when you think no one is looking. I love your optimism, your idealism, and your kisses. I love your dedication and loyalty to your family and how it's made me want to have a family of my own. Something I thought I never wanted, but deep down, truly did. My whole life, I felt like something was missing, and I found it when I met you. Enough?"

"For now." He kissed each of her fingertips, and tingles shot up her arm. "Say you'll give me a chance. I'll do whatever it takes. Even if you never want to get married, I don't care as long as we can be together forever."

Kelsey's heart swelled with joy. "I like the sound of forever."

"Me, too."

"You might not want to get used to having a bare ring finger."

"Excuse me?"

"Well, your family has a pretty good record when it comes to marriage, so that might make up for my parents. And since your parents can't adopt me, this is probably my only chance to become a member of your family. Kelsey Armstrong Waters Addison has a nice ring to it. I'm sure I could think of other reasons if you give me a few minutes."

He laughed. "I thought you were only taking baby steps right now."

She shrugged. "I feel lucky. I did catch the bouquet at my cousin Christina's wedding, so I'm the next to wed. And since you happen to be a firm believer in tradition…"

"Does this mean you'd…would you…?" He brushed his hand through his hair. "Who am I kidding? We've never even been on a date."

"True, but we've planned a wedding together. That has to count for at least three to six months of dating."

"I'd say a year."

"I've never dated anyone for a year, so I'll have to take your word for it." She grinned. "So…?"

"This is insane."

"I'm new at this sort of thing, but isn't love normally insane?"

"In this case, yes." He raised her right hand and kissed the top of it. "Kelsey Armstrong Waters, would you marry me?"

She stared at him. "I only plan for this to happen once, and I want everything to be perfect. Well, as perfect as we can get it. Do you think you could get down on one knee and try again?"

He smiled. "Anything else?"

"I don't suppose you have a carriage pulled by white horses outside and a dozen red roses? Or a slice of lemon cake handy?"

"Sorry. We can wait."

"No, we can't." She sat on the edge of the bed, her legs hanging over the side. Midas simply scooted back up beside her. "I'm ready now."

Will kneeled and took her hand in his. "Marry me, Kelsey. Be my wife and let me be your husband."

The words were music to her ears, candy to her mouth. She let them sink in. Closing her eyes, she sighed.

"Kelsey? Are you okay?"

"I'm savoring the moment."

"Don't forget about the guy on his knee waiting for an answer."

She opened her eyes. "I'm done savoring."

"And?"

"Yes." She smiled. "I'll marry you."

He rose, pulled her into his arms, and kissed her. "What do you say we get married tomorrow?"

She was dizzy from his proposal, from his kiss. "Tomorrow? Isn't that a little fast?"

"I doubt we could plan a wedding any more perfect for us."

That was the truth. She might be able to borrow Faith's dress. It fit, after all. The familiar scent of roses filled the room. "Do you smell that?"

"What?"

"It's nothing." Nothing but a sign marrying Will was the right thing to do. Not that she needed anything except her heart to tell her what to do. "A Valentine's wedding would be romantic."

"I can think of something even more romantic."

"What's that?"

"A Valentine's honeymoon."

"What about a happily-ever-after ending?"

He kissed her. "That's a given."

"Promise?"

"I promise."

Group Chat #4

Kelsey: *This is late notice, but I'm getting married tomorrow on Valentine's Day in Lake Tahoe!*

Serena: *Who is this and what have you done with our Kelsey?*

Kelsey: *It's me. If you don't believe me, you kissed Rupert before he kissed you because you weren't sure it would happen otherwise.*

Serena: *I'm convinced you're Kelsey, but you don't believe in marriage.*

Jane: *What's his name? Someone must have changed your mind.*

Kelsey: *His name is Will Addison, and he's the most amazing man. I love him so much.*

Elle: *This is what happens when you catch the bridal bouquet.*

Serena: *Might have to try harder to catch the next one.*

Jane: *I'm so happy for you, K.*

Elle: *Same.*

Serena: *Thrilled, but I'm bummed. I have two dress*

fittings tomorrow that I can't miss. I'm so sorry.

Jane: *I have to work.*

Elle: *I just can't swing it this fast. Sorry.*

Kelsey: *I understand, but I wanted you to know.*

Serena: *We'll do a post-wedding shower.*

Jane: *And bachelorette party.*

Elle: *Oh, we'll get you a bouquet to toss, too. That way, the odds will be more in our favor.*

Kelsey: *Thanks. And yes to all of that. Plus, you have to meet Will!*

EPILOGUE

February 14, Valentine's Day

Today was Kelsey's wedding day.

Starr had been so gracious about the switch from Faith's wedding to her and Bill's anniversary party to Will and Kelsey's wedding. She even told Will, "I told you so," which he graciously acknowledged with a kiss on her cheek, and "You're always right, Mom."

Now, Kelsey stood at the top of the staircase, her father at her side. The mahogany banister was decorated with a garland of flowers, greenery, and twinkling white lights. It was just as romantic as she'd imagined it would be the first time she stepped into Will's—soon-to-be-their—house. The sweet scent of the roses on the garland and in her bouquet tickled her nose, and she smiled.

It *was* almost time.

The din of the wedding guests, along with the music from the string quartet, rose from the living room. She wanted to pinch herself to make sure this wasn't a dream, but she didn't want to snag the lace fabric of her gown. Faith had graciously offered the use of her wedding dress last night, and Kelsey had accepted without a moment's hesitation, brushing aside any concerns about whether alterations would be needed. As far as she was concerned, no one except Christina and, one day soon, Will would ever know she'd tried on the dress before.

Christina.

She'd wanted to attend, but traveling such a long way with morning sickness would have been too much for her. Kelsey knew that her cousin would be with her in spirit and watching the livestream of the wedding, accompanying her every step of the way down the aisle.

There's something about the magical power of love.

Christina had said that once. Kelsey had rolled her eyes then. She believed now. Perhaps a sprinkle of magic had traveled all the way from San Montico. How else could she explain everything that had happened these past two weeks? That was about to happen…

With Christina, Serena, Jane, and Elle unable to be here, Kelsey asked Will's sisters to be in the wedding party. Her maid of honor, Faith, and her matron of honor, Hope, descended the staircase to the strains of "Canon in D." The song wasn't the most original when it came to processional music, but Kelsey didn't care. It had always been one of her favorites. That was all that mattered today. *She* was the bride.

Faith and Hope turned the corner. A few moments later, a new song began—Mozart's "Romance for String Quartet." Each note was like a kiss, rising to greet Kelsey.

This is it.

"Even though you'll be a married woman, you'll always be my little girl." Her father, Charles Waters, kissed her cheek. "Are you ready, sweetheart?"

Kelsey smiled, delighted her brother and her parents had dropped everything and flown to Nevada for her impromptu wedding. "I'm ready."

Each step brought her closer to her groom, to her new life, and she couldn't wait. She and her father rounded the corner. At the front of the living room standing before the fireplace were the minister, her brother, Cade, and Will.

Will.

She should have known he would look great in a tuxedo. He would look great in anything. Or nothing. She'd find out tonight. Kelsey grinned.

Will's wide smile softened. She felt so cherished, so loved. She never wanted this moment to end. Everything she'd never realized she'd wanted—*needed*—was right in front of her.

As she made her way down the makeshift aisle, his gaze never left hers. Forty-six other people waited in the living room they'd turned into a wedding chapel, but she barely noticed their presence.

The love shining in Will's eyes took Kelsey's breath

away. Warmth, joy, and euphoria filled her heart and her soul. The depth of the emotions and the intensity of the feelings overwhelmed her. And she loved it. This was what life was all about.

She heard her father say, "Her mother and I," but Kelsey hadn't heard the minister ask his question. She'd been too focused on the magic of the moment.

Her father kissed her cheek and placed her hand in Will's. Will gave it a gentle squeeze. His gaze held hers. She didn't want to look away. Ever. She saw her future in his eyes. A future full of love, laughter, family. A future with a happily-ever-after.

* * *

Will couldn't take his eyes off her.

He'd never seen a more stunning bride in his life.

Wearing the breathtaking vintage dress, headpiece, and veil, Kelsey glowed, a radiant light that poured through her smile, her eyes, everything. He grinned.

"Kelsey and Will have written wedding vows of their own," the minister announced to the friends and family gathered in the living room. "Kelsey."

She stared into Will's eyes. "I, Kelsey Armstrong Waters, take you, William Drake Addison, to be my husband. Today, in front of our family and friends, I pledge my love and fidelity."

This wonderful, intelligent woman was going to be *his* wife. Awe mixed with pride. He was the luckiest guy in the world.

Her eyes glimmered as she continued with the vows. Suddenly, she faltered, her voice clogging with emotion. "…and s-s-stay by your side in good times and in bad."

A single tear ran down her cheek, and a lump formed in Will's throat. She was so beautiful. He caressed her cheek, brushing the happy tears away.

She smiled. "I—I promise to listen to you, to laugh with you, to love you…"

Only two nights ago, she'd said those same words right here in his living room. So much…no, everything had changed since then. And he couldn't be happier.

Her eyes brimmed with tears. "…all the days of my life."

It was his turn. "Today, in front of our family and friends, I pledge my love and my fidelity. I promise to be your husband, your lover, and your friend. I will honor you, respect you, cherish you."

Will didn't know how he remembered the words and managed to say them without making a total fool of himself, but he drew strength from Kelsey. From her presence. From her smile. Each word meant so much to him, and Kelsey's tears showed him she felt the same way.

The time arrived for the ring exchange. Kelsey held the band of gold with her fingertips. "With this ring, I thee wed."

Her hand trembled as she slid the ring onto his finger. The look of pure joy in her eyes touched his soul, and he felt whole. One hundred percent complete.

Time to pull himself together, or he was never going to get the matching gold band on her finger. He swallowed. Hard. "With this ring, I thee wed."

* * *

With Will at her side, Kelsey watched the guests eat, drink, dance, and be merry. The same things guests did at any reception, but this one was different because it was *her* wedding. Those were her guests. And Will was her husband.

Husband.

She really liked the sound of that.

The clinking of silverware against glasses had Will leaning over to kiss her. They'd kissed so many times since the wedding ceremony, she'd lost count. Now, to keep it up tomorrow and the next day and the next.

"I could get used to doing this," he said.

She grinned. "I'm counting on it."

"The only thing left on your schedule is the bouquet and garter toss," Will whispered. "What do you say we toss them and get out of here?"

"That's the best offer I've had all night."

As the single women gathered on the dance floor, Kelsey noticed Faith hadn't joined them, so she had Cade bring her forward. Much to Faith's dismay.

Oh, well. What are the odds?

With Will at her side, she turned around and tossed the bouquet over her shoulder. The crowd gasped. Kelsey turned to see who the lucky woman was. What she saw was a very red-faced, angry Faith, holding the bouquet in front of her as if it were a dirty, smelly diaper.

"You know what this means, don't you?" Kelsey smiled at Will. "Faith will be the next one to get married."

He laced his fingers with Kelsey's, his brand-new shiny band of gold brushing her finger. Poor Faith. She didn't stand a chance. Kelsey chuckled.

Will kissed her. Short, but oh-so sweet. "Don't get your hopes up, my love."

My love. She sighed. "I have a feeling it's out of Faith's hands now."

"I hate to be the one to say it, but I've come to the conclusion my youngest sister will never get married."

"Never say never." Kelsey grinned, but to hedge her bet, she would do the bouquet toss with her three friends. Getting married had been the last thing she wanted. Now, look at her. There was still hope for Faith, someday. "Trust me on this one, okay?"

* * * * *

Thanks for reading *The Wedding Planner's Secret.* I hope you enjoyed Kelsey and Will's story. If you want to read the next book in the Wedding Bliss series, *The Dress Designer's Promise,* featuring Serena James, you can find it at melissamcclone.com/wedding-bliss-series.

If you want to know more about Kelsey's brother, Cade, his book is called *The Island Adventure* and is the first in my Billionaire Matchmaker series. You can find it at melissamcclone.com/books. It's a spinoff from my Billionaires of Silicon Forest series.

Join my newsletter to receive a FREE story and hear about upcoming and new releases, sales, freebies, and giveaways. Just go to melissamcclone.com/subscribe.

I appreciate your help spreading the word. Please tell a friend who loves sweet romance about this book and leave a review on your favorite book site. Reviews help readers find books!

Thanks so much!

ABOUT THE AUTHOR

USA Today bestselling author Melissa McClone has written over sixty sweet contemporary romance and women's fiction novels. She lives in the Pacific Northwest with her husband. She has three young adult children, a spoiled Norwegian Elkhound, and cats who think they rule the house. They do!

If you'd like to find Melissa online:
www.melissamcclone.com
www.facebook.com/melissamcclonebooks
www.facebook.com/groups/McCloneTroopers

Other Books by Melissa McClone

The Beach Brides/Indigo Bay Miniseries

Prequels to the Berry Lake Cupcake Posse series…

Jenny
Sweet Do-Over
Sweet Holiday Wishes
Sweet Yuletide
Sweet Beginnings
Indigo Bay Collection

The Berry Lake Cupcake Posse Series

Can five friends save their small town's beloved bakery?

Cupcakes & Crumbs
Kittens & Kisses
Tiaras & Teacups
Wishes & Weddings

Standalone Berry Lake Christmas Book

The Last Cottage on Pinewood Lane

Silver Falls Series

The Andrews siblings find love in a small town in WA state.

The Christmas Window
A Cup of Autumn
A Slice of Summer
A Sprinkle of Spring

One Night to Forever Series

Can one night change your life, and your relationship status?

Fiancé for the Night
A Little Bit Engaged
The Wedding Lullaby
Love on the Slopes
The One Night To Forever Box Set

The Billionaires of Silicon Forest

Who will be the last single man standing?

The Wife Finder
The Gold Digger
The Wish Maker
The Kiss Catcher
The Deal Breaker
The Game Changer
The Bet Makers (Newsletter exclusive)
The Billionaires of Silicon Forest Prequels
The Billionaires of Silicon Forest Series

Mountain Rescue Series

Finding love in Hood Hamlet
with a little help from Christmas magic…

His Christmas Wish
Her Christmas Secret
Her Christmas Kiss
His Second Chance
His Christmas Family

Her Royal Duty

Royal romances with charming princes and dreamy castles...

The Accidental Princess
The Reluctant Princess
The Not-So-Proper Princess
The Proper Princess

Quinn Valley Ranch

Two books featuring siblings in a multi-author series...

Carter's Cowgirl
Summer Serenade
Quinn Valley Ranch Two Book Set

A Keeper at Heart Series

These men know what they want, and love isn't on their list.
But what happens when each meets a keeper?

The Groom
The Soccer Star
The Boss
The Husband
The Date
The Tycoon

For the complete list of books, go to
melissamcclone.com/books

www.ingramcontent.com/pod-product-compliance
Lightning Source LLC
Chambersburg PA
CBHW020801190726
48285CB00006B/2119

* 9 7 8 1 9 4 4 7 7 7 8 4 5 *